The Whistling Man

By

Will Savive

Del-Grande Publishing
Hackensack, New Jersey
Copyright © 2020 Will Savive/Del-Grande
Publishing

ISBN: 978-0-578-80159-9
ASIN: B08NTW1MDK

The Whistling Man

Copyright © 2020 by Will Savive

For all things "Whistling Man," or to get exclusive deals and Whistling Man 2 release dates and content, please visit:

https://thewhistlingman-savive.com/

ISBN-13: 978-0-578-80159-9
BISAC: Horror/Thriller

Printed in the United States of America

The Whistling Man

Chapter 1

The young boy sat at the kitchen table.

"What do you want for dinner, El Silbón?" his mother asked.

The boy sat; stone faced. No expression; almost in a trance-like state. His mother only inches away, in their very small kitchen. She was putting wood in the stove. That stove was their prize possession. The family, of little means, had only purchased the old wood-burning stove—and the variety of cheap enamelware—just a few years earlier, in 1941. Saving up money from many years of hard labor by the man of the house, working at the farm.

The mother, Astrid, loved her only

child. However, it was more out of a sense of duty rather than traditional motherly love. She had grown increasingly impatient with his petulance, among other things. Astrid always sensed that something was wrong with the boy. Something was off. 'Was he even mine?' she sometimes wondered. No one in her family had ever acted like this. It must have been someone on her husband's side. The child's attitude had degenerated significantly over the last year. At one point she even expressed to her husband that the child might be possessed. She had gone as far as to suggest that the town priest pay a visit. There were times when he seemed normal, which made it that much more confusing. But there were just too many times that he acted more like a precocious, cantankerous adult rather than a ten-year old boy. His nature and aura felt dark to the mother.

His father, on the other hand, just didn't see it. He was their only son. 'This was just a phase,' he thought. This issue caused dissention between the couple. But the father worked long hours, and the day-to-day struggle took precedence over any other issues that they may have had. Moreover, the mother spent more time with the boy. She witnessed things that the father was not privy to. Even when she told him, he just shrugged it off. He wrote it off to the mother's poor perception and the stress the family was under to keep afloat. In any case, it caused a rift between the two.

Before she could ask her son again, she dropped the spoon she had been holding. She bent down to pick it up, right next to the side of the oven, by the metal model and serial number imprinted on the side that read, '27-12-A (42891).'

"Did you hear me El Silbón? I said, what do you want for dinner?" Just then the boy's father walks in the room.

"What's all the commotion in here?" he asked in a jolly voice.

"Hi hun! You're home early," she says. Then she gives him a kiss on the lips.

"It started to rain so we packed up early today."

"What about the pay, Sergio?" his

wife asked with concern. She had moved to the large steel pot filled with water to wash her hands.

"I will make it up tomorrow, no worries," the father responded. "Hey little man. How are you?" he asks. But the boy does not respond. He just stares forward. "What's for dinner?"

"I was going to make chicken," the wife retorts. "But the child will not tell me what he wants to eat."

"El Silbón, tell your mother what you want to eat, son," his father said.

"I want the guts of a deer," El Silbón says loudly. His mother looks at her husband with confusion.

"But sweety," the mother says, "don't you want something a bit more appetizing?"

"No!" he shouts. "I want the guts of a deer, I said!"

"Ma, surely you can make it taste good if I go out and get a deer," the father says.

"But you have worked so hard all day," she says.

4

"It's okay. I will be back shortly." The boy had become quite adroit at exploiting his father's acquiescent nature.

Sergio grabbed his jacket, his rifle, and a bottle of liquid doe urine and headed out into the night to find a deer.

Venezuela is typically characterized by warm weather. Because it's located just north of the equator, temperatures do not fluctuate wildly, and it generally enjoys a balmy, warm climate. Coastal regions are even balmier, with these lowland areas enjoying a year-round tropical climate. The seasons are categorized best in two parts: a dry season and a rainy season. The dry season runs from mid-December to mid-April. The rainy season runs from late April to mid-November. The rainy season is actually the most sultry and unpleasant.

However, with the vastness of the territory, there are regions that do not comply with this seasonal concept. In areas where there are mountainous ranges, temperatures can get quite cold. In fact, elevated areas in Venezuela, such as the Andes Mountains, reach more than 16,000 feet. Snow-capped peaks can be witnessed year-round in this rugged mountain system. For every 1,000 feet of elevation brings a drop of approximately five-degrees. And Pavoso is no different. Pavoso sits about 12,000 feet above sea level, on a plateau in the middle of the vaunted Capella Mountains. The weather here is typically between 18°- and 38°-degrees Fahrenheit.

This particular October day was on the colder side.

Sergio was sure to bundle up. He had his scarf, he wore his gloves, and he had on his red and black checkered hunting cap, as he always did; the one lined with fur and extending below his ears. All kinds of wildlife lived in the surrounding forest and the mountains beyond. The list includes the grey wolf, the red fox, the pika, the wooly hare, deer, mountain cats, mountain lions, bears, and more. The farm land needed to be fenced-in, in order to keep out the abundance of wildlife that lived and traveled through the area. For this adventure, Sergio would most likely have to battle the mountainous region in order to bring home a prized deer.

Three inches of snow covered the greenery in every direction. It was forecasted to snow later that night, even. Sergio had gone on similar hunts since he was a child. Very rarely did he come back empty handed. Sergio always followed the same two routes when hunting. It all depended upon which way the wind was blowing. He always wanted to walk against the wind, so that the animals did not smell him coming. On this day the wind was blowing west, so Sergio made a right after leaving the cabin and entered the woods there. He would walk on the south side of town traveling east.

Sergio creeps slowly and carefully through the brush as he walks east, making sure to make as little noise as possible. He is on his way to his usual spot, perched up the mountain ridge, in order to get the best vantage point. There, he will sit and wait. But before he could get there, he spots a grazing deer and her two-little fawns. He spots the deer grazing about 50-yards away. Sergio gets into position to take the shot.

The hoot of a horned owl breaks the silence. Seconds later the howl of a wolf. Then, several wolves howl back. They are telling their pack that they have made a kill and it's feeding time. Sergio steadies his rifle on a big rock in front of him. He purposely slows his breathing as he gently presses his eye against the scope of the rifle. He carefully sets the cross-hair of the rifle on the heart of the deer.

The deer looks up quickly. A low noise nearby has her looking for danger. With none that the deer can see, its head falls back down quickly and continues eating. He holds steady for a few seconds, trying to ensure that his aim is precise.

BANG!

A loud shot rings through the night. Nearby birds scatter in different directions. The blast, so loud that Sergio's ear plugs are the only protection from him losing his short-term hearing. The shot hurls quickly toward the mother deer. Before the mother deer even knew what had happened, the bullet had narrowly missed her, passing just underneath her belly and hitting the ground a few feet away. The mother deer looked up in confusion. She took a moment to gather herself. Then, she darted out of sight within seconds. Her young children followed close behind her.

Sergio rarely ever misses. 'What had just happened?' he thought. It would turn out to be a very costly miss.

Sergio waited there for another half hour. With no other deer in site, he decided to go to another spot that was high in deer traffic. He walked further east, toward the water. This time he poured some of the doe urine on a tree that was in the line of fire from his second perch. He waited and waited, but no deer ever came. He tried one other area, but again, he had no luck. He returned home after two-hours of hunting with nothing.

He was exhausted!

El Silbón had been waiting outside for his father to return for about 15 minutes, wearing only a t-shirt in the blistering cold. Sergio was very upset that he did not deliver for his son. As Sergio approached his son his shoulders slumped and his head faced the ground.

"I'm so sorry son," said Sergio. "I searched near and far, but I could not capture a deer." El Silbón's eyes filled with water, his inside with rage. His face turned red and he clenched his teeth together. Sergio could not even look his son in the eyes.

"I told you I wanted the guts of a deer!" he screams loudly. Sergio expected that exact response. He hated disappointing his son.

"I'm so sorry," he said again. Sergio held up both hands half way, palms facing the sky, then dropped them. He walked toward the house shaking his head side to side, obsessing about the shot he had missed. 'If he had just raised the rifle an inch, pre-shot,' he thought, 'the outcome would have been very different.' The time he would have saved and the happiness he would have brought his son weighed on him heavily.

El Silbón, in an uncontrollable rage, grabs the large machete that was stuck in a piece of log that lay on the ground. As if possessed, El Silbón gripped the handle of the blade tightly and rushed his father. Running toward his father, El Silbón raises the machete in a swinging motion. Just as his father turns, El Silbón is bringing the machete down from over his head with both hands. The blade hummed as he brought it down. Stunned, confused, and unable to process what was happening, Sergio watches as a good portion of the front blade is thrust into his chest. The blade tears through flesh and strikes bone.

"I told you I wanted the guts of a deer," El Silbón shouts again, as he pulls the machete from his father's chest. A brief squelching sound emanates as he pules the blade from his father's flesh. What seemed like in the same motion, the b oy strikes his father again with another blow to the chest. Sergio screams, and falls to his knees.

"Son, what are you doing?" he shouts in anguish. Before he could finish the sentence, El Silbón swings the machete again at his father's chest. This time his father puts his hands up to block the blow. The sharp blade tears right through his fingers. The force of the blade severs three fingers from his left hand and two from his right cleanly on its way to the chest yet again. The snow quickly turns blood-red in the area of the attack. Over and over El Silbón swings the blade at his father until his eyes shut and he lay on his back, barely breathing and gasping, inadvertently, for air.

Back in the kitchen, his mother had just started boiling potatoes. She had waited a while to start cooking them in an attempt to have everything ready at the same time. El Silbón walks in the kitchen with both hands filled with slimy guts. He is covered in blood from head to toe.

"Here mama," he says. "Here is dinner."

"Where did you get this from," she asked in confusion.

"From Daddy," he answered politely.

"And where did he get them from?" she asked.

"He grew them inside his belly," he responded.

With a look of terror, his mother ran

from the kitchen. As she ran past her son she asked, "What did you do?" She ran furiously to the front door, which was ajar. A trail of blood led to the front yard. Only ten-feet outside the door she saw her husband lying on his back. His stomach had been ripped open and he had been gutted like a pig. Tears welled up in her eyes. "No, no," she screamed. "What have you done? What have you done, demon child?"

El Silbón stood silently in the doorway. He then turned, emotionless, and went back inside the house. His mother ran back in and went upstairs to the spare bedroom.

"Pappa!" she shouted. "Pappa!" She opened the door to her father's room. "Come quickly! El Silbón has done a terrible thing. I told you all he was the child of the devil." After El Silbón's grandfather, Zuma, saw the carnage; he overpowered the ten-year-old boy and dragged him to a tree that stood twenty-yards from the house. Zuma tied him to the tree, stomach first. Zuma was a descendant of the Aztecs, a Mesoamerican people of central Mexico in the 14th, 15th and 16th centuries. Zuma's parents migrated to Venezuela when he was a young boy. Although, today the descendants of the Aztecs are referred to as the Nahua, Zuma and his family continued to practice and recognize the Aztec culture. Zuma was, in fact, the father of the man that El Silbón had just murdered. El Silbón's mother was a native of Venezuela.

Once Zuma had the boy tied to the tree, he began chanting, "Ah-wee-ah-teh-tay-o. Ah-wee-ah-teh-tay-o." His eyes appeared to roll around the back of his head, as he chanted the ancient curse on the boy. He had a large brush in his hand. The handle was made of wood. The bristles on the brush were dark, long and stiff, and made from the hair of a badger. At his feet was a can of blood. Zuma had drained a portion of his son's blood into the can. Zuma bent down and dipped the brush into the blood. Then, he slowly rose again. "Ah-wee-ah-teh-tay-o. Ah-wee-ah-teh-tay-o," Zuma chanted. Then, he flicked the blood onto the boy. He chanted, "Ah-wee-ah-teh-tay-o," two times before flicking blood onto the boy. He repeated this for some time, before kneeling and whispering quietly to the Gods for several minutes.

When he was done, he picked up a large whip and began whipping the boy's back. One lash after another, he hit the boy with all of the rage in him. The boy screamed in pain. "I will get you for this," the boy vowed, as the skin on his back was hanging off. After nearly 50 lashes, Zuma stopped. He grabbed a wooden bowl filled with lemon juice. He slowly poured it on the boy's wounds. The boy bellowed in pain. Zuma again chanted, "Ah-wee-ah-teh-tay-o," as he did so. The boy screamed so loud from the pain that it echoed in the valley. When he was done, he untied the boy from the tree. His lifeless body fell to the ground like a block of wood. His mother watched from inside, through the family room window. The boy looked over at her, helplessly. "Mama," he mouthed. Too weak to make much of a sound. His mother turned from the window and walked deeper into the house and out of sight.

Zuma pulled the boy to his feet. He

handed him a bag. "Here," he said, as he forced it into the boy's hands. His grip could barely hold it. "This is a bag with one of your father's bones. Take this and leave this place immediately!" The boy cried, "But grandpa..." The gravity of the situation had certainly sunk into the boy's head by now. He didn't know what he had done wrong, he only knew that he was going to pay the ultimate price for it.

Before he could finish his statement, Zuma smacked him in the face. "Leave here now!" he yelled. "And never return!" The boy walked off into the woods. He walked for hours, aimlessly. Tired and cold, he stopped to lean on a tree. Just when he thought he had a moment of rest he heard a menacing snarl. He turned and saw four hungry, wild dogs with their fangs exposed. All were staring at the boy as if he was their next meal. The boy ran, still holding the sack tightly. But he was tired, and no match for the hungry dogs. They caught up to him after only a few steps. One jumped on his back. Another gnawed on his leg. The boy fell forward. Another pounced. Soon all four were chewing on his flesh. He screamed, to no avail. But they stopped prematurely. One even winced. Abruptly, they all ran away at the same time, like scared puppies. The boy laid there motionless. His eyes suddenly opened; his face in the snow. For him to live more than five-minutes would be a miracle. How was he even alive, still? The sky began to rumble. The earth started shaking. The arm of a skeleton reached out of the sea, with a fist of fury held high. The boy sat up, mechanically—like a robot. His eyes, glowing. The next morning, the boy was nowhere to be found. And his mother and grandfather were found gruesomely slaughtered in their home.

Chapter 2

2019 – Phoenix, AZ

Harry opened the door like a bat out of hell.

"Are you guys ready for the trip of a lifetime?" he asked excitedly. His best friend, Brian, was sitting on the couch watching TV. Brian's wife, Sarah, was carrying a red duffle bag. She placed it by the front door.

"If he [Brian] would get off his ass and help we might be ready a bit faster."

"Hun!" Brian exclaimed. "I'm catching up on the news, since we won't get news in English where we're going." Harry grabs two of the suitcases that Sarah had left at the bottom of the stairs. He drops them by the front door.

"Oh God, him [Brian] and his politics," she says, as she rolls her eyes.

"So, we are finally going to meet the flame of the week," Sarah says.

"No, no, this one is different," Harry says.

"Ok, like the last three girls," Sarah says sarcastically. Harry smirks and shrugs it off.

"This girl has class. She is very educated," said Harry.

"So, she is not the typical floozie we're used to? If I have to entertain another one like Tanya (Sarah accents the name in a funny slur, dragging out the name) while you idiots go off fishing, I swear I will kill you."

"Tanya was a gem hun," Brian says. "I remember she said she finished a puzzle in 5 months and couldn't understand why the box said 3-6 years." Sarah bursts out laughing.

"Yeah, she was so dumb, she tried

to climb Mountain Dew," Sarah joked.

"She was sick once and made an appointment with Dr. Pepper," Brian joked.

"Ha, ha, very funny," said Harry. "Well she was a fitness model, and could make a dead man cum, so things balanced out."

"Ew gross," Sarah cringed.

Brian's home is located on West Molly Lane in Phoenix, AZ. The house is located near the North Gateway in the Desert View neighborhood in Phoenix, Arizona. It is a highly affluent suburb that offers residents a dense suburban feel, highly rated schools, and prides itself on its politically conservative views. More than 72-percent of Desert View families own their homes. Leaving only a small percentage of renters compared to many other areas of the country.

Brian and Sarah have been married for seven-years, and have no children. They dated for two-years prior to getting married. Brian and Harry have been best friends since high school. Harry, a writer, is a trust fund baby, as they call it. He has enjoyed the fruits of a very wealthy family of doctors and bankers. Harry is known as the "black sheep" of the family for not following a long line of prosperous careers. His family shunned his insolence, but still provide him with all the necessary resources to afford his lavish lifestyle. And being an only child made it even more fruitful for him.

Brian, a very successful attorney, and Sarah, a likewise successful prosecutor, have carved out a piece of heaven for themselves. They both work very hard, and both find Harry's lifestyle quite entertaining. Deep down they think of Harry's hedonistic adventures and frivolous, non-committal dating life to be a cautionary tale. Something they would not aspire to. Yet, despite their constant cajoling, Harry is happy living the single life. Wooing all types of women with his charm, good looks, good humor, and of course enormous inheritance. Harry is quite generous. He spares no expense on a good time for himself and his friends. And despite his monetary status, Harry is very down to earth when it comes to viewing others, which is more like an equal than a subservient. Although, his status could go to his head from time to time.

Brian rises up from the couch and walks over to Harry.

"So, what exactly is the plan, Stan?" he asks.

"Well, as you know we are heading to Caracas to sign the papers for the house my father left me. I figured we could spend the first night there."

"I read that Caracas is the richest area in Venezuela. I didn't know your father owned a house there. You never mentioned it," Sarah says.

"Neither did I," Harry says, followed by a chuckle. "I only found out after the reading of the will, which annoyingly was just a month ago."

"I can't believe it took almost a year after your father's death, God bless his soul (Brian does the sign of the cross), before they tell you this stuff."

"I know," Harry responds. "Well, you are a lawyer," Harry says to Sarah. "You should know this."

"I'm a federal prosecutor, not a

private client lawyer."

"So, what else is planned on this trip, Harry," Brian asks. "Why so secretive about it?"

"Just get your stuff together for seven days that you will never forget. You know me, when I plan it, it's always better than you think."

"This is true," Brian responds. Sarah nods her head in agreement. She couldn't argue with that. Everyone knew Harry threw the best parties and coordinated the best trips. He just has a knack for it and a flare for a good time and the finer things.

Harry's phone receives a text notification.

"It's her!" he exclaims excitedly. "She's here! Be nice Sarah," said Harry.

Sarah rolls her eyes. Harry rushes to the door, almost in a full sprint. Once he gets outside, he saunters over to greet Laurie. Brian and Sarah rush to the window to get a look see. Harry walks out the door and around the three big cacti planted in front of the house. A Black Range Rover and a Silver Mercedes C600 are parked, side-by-side, closest to the garage door of the enormous driveway. Harry's silver 2020 Bugatti Centodieci is parked behind the Range Rover.

Pulling into the driveway slowly at that moment was a Volvo XC40 SUV. Harry approaches the vehicle on the driver's side. The window slowly slides down.

"Did you find it okay?" Harry asks.

"Yeah, this GPS thing is a wonder," she says. The beautiful, girl-next-door type woman opens the door and exits the vehicle. Harry approaches and kisses her on the lips.

"Hey hun, so glad you are here," he says with delight.

"Me too," she says. "This should be interesting." They both walk inside the house.

"Guys, I would like you to meet the lovely and talented, Laurie," Harry says. "This is Brian." They both shake hands and say, "Nice to meet you."

"And this is Sarah, but don't believe a word she says about me. She has temporary brain damage." Sarah hits Harry in his arm. Harry flinches away in fear, anticipating the blow. Laurie smiles.

"I'm sure she has more brains than you," Laurie says. "Hi, I'm *Laurie Orsted.*" Sarah goes in for a kiss on the cheek and a hug.

"I like this one already," Sarah says.

"Can I get you something to drink?" Sarah asks Laurie.

"Sure," she responds. The two women head into the kitchen.

"Wow, she is pretty, man," Brian says. "Not your typical woman."

"What does that mean?" Harry asks.

"I just mean she seems very wholesome looking. Normal looking, you know?" Harry laughs.

"Funny," he responds. The women come out of the kitchen. Laurie is holding a bottle of water.

"We'd better get going," Harry says. "We have a long trip."

"Whose car are we going to take?" Brian asks.

"I think we should all travel together, probably in the Range Rover" Brian suggests.

"Not necessarily," Harry says. "Look!" Harry brings them to the window that faces the front of the home.

"Wohhh!" Brian exclaims.

Sitting in front of the house was an 18 passenger 2014 white Range Rover Stretch Limo.

"I got it cause, you know; Sarah loves her Range Rover so much," Harry says, winking at Sarah.

"Remember what I said to you in the kitchen?" Sarah says to Laurie. "Forget it, he's a keeper," she continues. Laurie laughs.

Both couples happily entered the limo for the ride to the airport; Laurie next to Harry, Sarah next to Brian. Both couples faced each other, sitting on opposite sides of the vehicle.

"I would like to propose a toast," said Harry. He raises a bottle of champaign.

"It's bad luck to toast with champaign until we get to the house," Brian says.

"Bry, since when have any of us had bad luck?" Harry says, laughing.

"Look at our lives. It doesn't get any better than this, and it isn't getting any worse. Not where we are going, at least. That I can assure you. Now raise your glasses. To the trip of a lifetime."

All four glasses meet in the middle and cling together.

"To the trip of a lifetime," they all echoed.

It was a thirty-two-minute drive to *SkyRanch at Carefree*, a private airport in the middle of the desert. Harry had rented a private jet for the flight to Caracas, Venezuela. Because the time in Caracas is the same as the time in New York, and because Arizona is the Mountain Time Zone; they will lose three-hours once they arrive in Caracas.

The drinks were flying. From the limo to the plane, plane to the final destination; it was clear to everyone that they were on vacation. What made it better was that Sarah and Laurie were getting along nicely. Laurie is a very down to earth woman. She is from modest means and has worked her way into a comfortable lifestyle. She is frugal with money, treats people kindly, and lives a modest, conservative lifestyle. Moreover, she is well educated in many areas, which impressed Brian a lot. Brian is an intellectual and loves to "shoot-the-shit," as he calls it, about any intellectual subject. Anytime he hears someone discussing intellectual subjects, such as politics, science, current events, etc., Brian will slide his way into the conversation. Even with strangers. Sarah thinks it's quite annoying and even pompous at times, but she loves her husband very much for the same qualities she finds annoying at times. Brian has toned it down somewhat, from his earlier days, although, you wouldn't know it from this conversation.

Just before they arrive at their final destination, the limo stops by an ally in the center of town.

"Wait here. I'll be right back," Harry says.

"Where are you going?" Sarah asks. Harry ignores her and hastily closes the door and heads up the ally. The others in the car are confused. Harry returns minutes later with a *blue duffle bag*. As he approaches the limo, the driver pops the trunk. Harry put the duffle bag in the trunk and hops back in the limo.

"What was that about?" Sarah asks.

"It's a surprise," Harry says nervously.

"What's in the bag?" Laurie asks.

"I said it's a surprise. No worries."

The limo pulls off, headed for the mansion.

Chapter 3

The Mansion

The jet landed at the *Simon Bolivar International Airport of Maiquetía*, an airport for private Jets located approximately 13 miles from downtown Maiquetía. Again, Harry had another stretch limousine waiting to take the group to Caracas, where the mansion is located. This time he chose a stretch-Cadillac. The ride to the house in Caracas was another thirty-minutes. When they arrived at the mansion, they came upon a small security booth with an armed guard inside.

After a brief orientation, the guard gave them the go-ahead. The gates opened slowly and the limo drove through.

"Oh, my word!" Brian says in excitement, with one foot on the ground, exiting the limo. "Look at this place."

"Wow, I don't think I ever wanna go home," Sarah expresses. All four of them exit in awe.

"This property is humongous. Look at the mountains. What a view," said Laurie. Harry remained silent. He just looked around with a thousand-yard-stare. The moment was overwhelming. It wasn't so much the cost of the property. He was worth millions already. It was the attention to detail and the aesthetic beauty he so much admired. And it was now his.

Walking toward the group was an attractive brunette woman with tan skin and a light grey skirt suit.

"Good afternoon, I'm Consuelo Áñez, the listing agent," she said, with a slight accent. "Welcome to Bella Feliz Mansion," she expressed with enthusiasm. "You must be Harry?" she says, as she attempts to shake hands.

"No, actually, I'm his friend Brian," he says, as their hands meet. Consuelo turns her head and locks eyes with Harry, as her hand goes limp in Brian's hand.

"I'm Harry." Consuelo breaks the grip of Brian's hand and immediately extends it to Harry.

"Oh, I'm so embarrassed. I must apologize. I'm so sorry." Being that Brian was dressed to impress and Harry was dressed so casually, one can easily surmise why Consuelo had made such an error.

"Think nothing of it, Cons-u-e-l-a, was it?"

"Consuelo," she says humbly, correcting Harry.

"Consuel-o?" Harry replies. "Doesn't the O mean male?" he asks. He looks at the group as if awaiting a laugh. But they just awkwardly smile. Sarah rolls her eyes. Laurie smacks him gently on the shoulder.

"Don't mind him," Laurie says.

"Wow," Harry says, "this place is everything I imagined and much more. You met Brian. This is his wife, Sarah [the two shake hands], and my girlfriend (he says clumsily), Laurie." Laurie looks at Harry and shrugs her shoulders, and then her and Consuelo shake hands and greet each other, likewise.

"If you would like, I can show you around?" Consuelo says.

"Sure, that would be great," Harry

replies. "This is like a small town," Harry jests. They walked toward the front door, led by Consuelo. Harry just behind her, grabs Laurie's hand. Laurie looks up at him with a smile. Brian and Sarah were trailing not far behind. Brian's head was swiveling, trying to keep up with the overload of visual stimuli.

"You believe this place?" Brian says quietly to Sarah.

"He is one lucky son of a bitch, let me tell you," Sarah replies.

Consuelo stops just before the front door. She turns around and faces the group.

"As you see when you arrived, there is a guardhouse prior to entering the solid electric gate. The guard will call you to announce any and all visitors. Obviously, he knew of your arrival, and you can notify him of any guests for quicker entry. Upon entering the complex, you are welcomed by a beautiful artificial waterfall, surrounded by greenery. And the lot just to the left, after entering the gate, fits forty cars comfortably."

Consuelo turns and opens the front door. They all enter. The house is fully furnished. Harry's father had purchased the home only recently before his death. Harry's father and mother had gotten a divorce years earlier. His mother lived in Arizona, not far from where Harry lived. His father had several homes, but lived primarily in Venezuela for only three-months before his sudden death.

"Everything breathes spaciousness and light," Consuela continued. "Notice the functional distribution of the spaces, the impeccable ceiling and the marble floors, except for the wood that covers them in the six rooms on the second floor. There are five bathrooms on that level that are immaculate, and an auxiliary kitchen, which is exquisite, and complements the main one on the ground floor."

Just then, Harry's phone rings.

"I'm sorry, please excuse me for a second," he said. "Hello? Yes, this is him."

The others continued to talk with Consuelo for the time being.

"Great, thank you," Harry said. "We should be there tomorrow afternoon at some point. No, [Harry chuckles], we don't have dogs. Yes, I'm sure. Enough with the dogs already! No, I said we won't be needing them! We are only staying one night. But... Just have the place ready." Harry hangs up and returns to the group.

"What was that all about," Sarah asks.

"Nothing," Harry responds. "I will explain later. Let's just get on with the tour." Seconds later, Harry, distracted, says, "You know what, Consuelo. Can we finish this tour another day? I need to take a shower and get settled in. We have a lot to do this week."

Confused, but compliant, Consuelo says, "Sure, Harry. You have my number. Just call me and I will come right out and continue the tour."

"What's wrong buddy," Brian says. "Is everything okay?"

"Yeah, yeah," Harry says. He walks over to a mini bar. "We have plenty of time for formalities. Right now, it's party time."

Brian looks at the ladies. "He has a point," he says.

"Shots?" Harry asks. Harry lines up four shots; Two Johnny Walker Black Label shots for the men and two Fireball shots for the ladies. Laurie goes into her bag and pulls out a blue-tooth speaker.

"How about some music?" she asks.

"Yes!" the other three shouted in unison. Within seconds, Laurie hits play and the song *Human Nature* from *Madonna* begins playing. Harry turns it up and starts dancing. Brian starts pouring drinks while shaking his shoulders to the music. Harry starts doing a seductive dance directed at Laurie. Sarah and Laurie both start laughing, as Harry's dancing skills—although in rhythm—would not be categorized as professional by any means. Clearly, he was trying to use himself to draw a laugh, as he often did.

Making the peace sign with his fingers, putting them sideways, and running them across his eyes; he sang in a whispering voice the beginning of the song.

"Express yourself, don't repress yourself."

The more the song played, the more uninhibited Harry became. He was feeling the freedom of the situation. He had, in an instant, almost doubled his net worth. He was the star of the moment. And, he would soak up every second of his fifteen-minutes. The females soon followed Harry in dance. However, their dancing was actually seductive. No one was taking themselves too seriously. While the women complimented Harry with their talented back-up dancing skills, Brian danced to each with a much-needed full drink. Brian's dance moves were much more awkward, and less rhythmic. But it mattered not.

Just before the song ended, six women in full maid outfits walked down the extravagant staircase. They stopped at the midway point, which was a roomy middle section, with stairs extending in two different directions. The maids appeared puzzled about what to do next. Laurie abruptly stopped the music. By now, Harry had his buttoned-down short sleeve Hawaiian shirt completely unbuttoned, and his hair was disheveled. He continued to sing a few words that would have followed if the music hadn't already been turned off.

"Hey!" he shouted. Laurie raised her chin, motioning for him to turn around. "Oh hey," Harry said. Brian spit out his drink with laughter. The head Maid spoke up.

"Do you require our services, sir?"

"I require you to go drink alcohol and listen to loud music for the remainder of the evening. And order Chinese food, or something, if you're hungry. And put it on my tab." The other three started laughing. "At ease," he shouted loudly. "Now put the music back on and pour more drinks!" He announced.

Laurie obliged with the song *Hypnotize*, by *The Notorious B.I.G.* And the dancing continued. Harry immediately gave his best impression of a rapper. He stuck his lips out and started moving his hands in chopping motions toward the ground. Simultaneously, with each chop, he raised a knee. When his left knee raised, his left hand chopped down and vice versa. The whole time, he shook his head repeatedly.

Chapter 4

Dinner in Caracas

Once the afternoon party died down a bit, the couples chose their rooms. Brian and Sarah took one of the upstairs guest bedrooms. It was a cozy spot that had a view of the tennis courts at the left end of the house. Harry and Laurie, of course, took the master bedroom, which was down the long hallway, facing the pool at the back of the house. The group had decided that they would go out to eat, and then go back to the mansion for a late-night party. The restaurant they decided on was *La Cocina Urrutia*, which serves traditional Spanish cuisine that offers the best of Venezuela's rich culinary culture. The restaurant is filled with contemporary art on the walls. It offers a large list of beguiling specialties, and is touted as the best cuisine in the region.

After they are seated, a male waiter comes over and introduces himself, in broken English, and reads them the specials. Once he is finished, Harry slips him a $100 USD.

"Take care of us, okay?" Harry says.

"Thank you, sir, thank you," he says, as he bows his head toward Harry.

"We would like two bottles of your finest wine, please," Brian says mockingly. Harry smiles and shakes his head up and down at the waiter. Laurie was taken by surprise by Brian's comment.

"He [Harry] always says that as soon as we sit down at a restaurant," Sarah tells Laurie.

"Hey, nothing less for my people,"

Harry says.

"Oh, now we're your people?" Sarah replies sarcastically. "Shall I go in the kitchen and help them prepare your meal, sire?" Sarah continues.

"Well," Harry says suggestively, while shrugging his shoulders. Sarah picks up her napkin and throws it at Harry, hitting him in the face. Laurie spits out the tiny bit of water that she had just begun to sip.

"Okay, I guess I deserved that," Harry says, as he hands her back her napkin.

"You guys are a riot," Laurie says in jest.

"So, what was that phone call about earlier?" Laurie asks Harry. "Something you said about being there tomorrow afternoon?"

"Very observant, Laurie," said Sarah.

"Please tell me we are going to the beach!" Brian exclaims. Harry takes a deep breath. "Ok, so here it goes," Harry pronounces. He leans in. "Aside from bringing you guys down here on a vacation, I also have a money-making opportunity for you."

"Oh, here we go," Sarah replies

sarcastically.

"Well, there's this village just south of here that I recently purchased."

"You bought a village?" Laurie asks in amazement.

"Yeah, I bought the land. And there is a great opportunity to turn it into a lot of money. Brian, I want you to come work with me as a partner on this." Brian's eyes sprout wide open.

"Me?" he asks. "What expertise do I have?"

"Yeah, what's the catch?" Sarah inquires.

"Well," Harry says. He sits back, takes a sip of wine, "it's a small-town south-west of here, called *Pavoso*. It's in between Valencia and Guanarito. It's a rich farming environment, and there are several places for small businesses to be developed."

"Wait, you said, 'to be developed?'" Brian asks.

"Well, it's kind of been abandoned," Harry equivocated.

"Kind of?" Laurie asks.

"One-hundred percent abandoned, to be exact," Harry responds.

"Oh, great. Why was that?" Sarah asks, with a suspicious look on her face.

"Something about an abandoned mine and some noxious chemical build-up that is believed to have contaminated the water and soil, or something."

"Or something?" Sarah pronounces. "You sound as if it's no big deal."

"Wow, Harry, I gotta say, that is a huge project to undertake," Brian explains. "There are a lot of moving parts to that."

"I'm sure there are," Harry says. "I want you to come and work with me on the project, Brian. With your scientific expertise and my money and people skills, we can make more money than we ever dreamed of."

"Harry, I appreciate the offer, but I can't just walk away from my career for some unknown project that certainly involves way more than you are bargaining for."

"Brian, you're an Environmental Engineer for the EPA. You tell me all the time that you wish you had more freedom. You are the most talented engineer anywhere, and you are being under-paid and under-appreciated. I'm offering you an opportunity of a lifetime."

"Harry, I have a stable job, great benefits, and I make a very good living there. I know nothing about this area or the problems with the mine."

Harry leans in again.

"Fair enough, which is why we are going there tomorrow to look at it and see what you think. Look, the bottom line is, I need you. I can't do this without you. I will double your salary and split the profits with you. Once we restore the land, we can sell it and turn a huge profit. Or we can build up the area and lease all the land to its new inhabitants. Build affordable homes and such, and have income forever. And you will never have to work again. All's I'm asking is that you take a look at the place and the situation. If you believe that something can come out of this than I will continue on with or without you, that's your choice. If you think it is unsalvageable than, hey, I'm out a few mil; no sweat, right?"

Everyone appears to take a deep breath. For a moment there is silence.

You could cut the tension with a

knife.

"Okay, I guess since you brought me all the way down here, I can take a look at it," Brian responds.

"Alright, Brian!" Harry exclaims.

"I think I need a shot after that," Laurie says. Everyone chuckles.

"I like this one, Harry," Sarah mentions.

"Andrés," Harry shouts. He had taken a peek at the waiter's name tag on his previous visit to the table. "Can we get a round of shots please, sir?"

"Oh," Harry says, "there is one other thing."

"I knew it," Sarah says suspiciously.

"The place is said to be haunted or something by some crazy, evil dude or something." Everyone starts laughing.

"That's what I said, exactly. The Realtor said that no one should go down there without at least two dogs. The fucker sounded serious to. He kept going on and on about it." Harry rolls his eyes and takes another swig of wine.

After desert, Andrés comes over to the table.

"Can I get you anything else?"

"What do you know about Pavoso?" Laurie asks.

"Pavoso?" he says apprehensively. "No, no. No good," Andrés replies, sounding alarmed at the thought.

"You know what we are talking about, the abandoned town?" Brian asked.

"Yes, yes. No good. Espíritu Maligno," he says.

"What's that?" Laurie asks.

"Evil Spirit," Harry says, knowing the little Spanish that he does.

"Yes, there is an evil spirit down there," Andrés says. "It roams the area, killing anyone it comes in contact with. Bad, bad place. It is why the people left the area."

Harry Laughs. "No, Andrés, they left the area because of contamination. We are going there tomorrow"

Andrés starts shaking his head quickly side to side. "No, no, sir, I say respectfully. Not contamination that drove them out. It was the evil spirit. Stay away, I tell you. Stay away!" Andrés says, looking very animated.

"Thank you, Andrés. That'll be all," Harry

says. "You see," said Harry. "These people are not that bright. They need a leader. We can do a lot of good here."

"I don't know, Harry," Laurie says. "That was pretty spooky. And he sounded pretty convincing."

"You're not suggesting that there is a monster or something down there, Laurie, are you?" asked Brian.

"Maybe not a monster, or whatever; but what about some crazy person or persons who are taking advantage of the area now that it has been abandoned?"

"Yeah," said Sarah, "that is a possibility."

"But you heard what he said," Harry emphasized. "He said that it was the reason it was abandoned."

"So, that would mean that the killer or killers would have been there prior to abandonment," Brian said, backing up Harry's philosophy on the matter.

"Well, all's I know is we need to be careful. And we should look around and make sure that the area is clear before we get settled in," Laurie said.

"Don't worry. Brian and I will sweep

the area and make sure you girls are safe. You know I will protect you at all costs, babe." Harry leaned over and kissed Laurie on the lips.

"Yeah, me to hun," said Brian. He leaned in, like Harry, and Kissed Sarah.

A Night at the Mansion

Once the group got back to the mansion the drinks continued to flow. Harry grabbed the notorious blue duffle bag from the living room closet that he had stuffed into the trunk of the limo hours earlier.

"Okay. So, you all wanted to know what was in the bag, so here it goes." Harry opens the bag and pulls out an all-black FN Five-sevenN USG handgun.

"Wow!" Laruie exclaims nervously.

"What the hell?" Sarah says angrily.

"Nice!" Brian cries joyfully.

"What is that for?" Laurie asks.

"You said you wanted protection, right? Well, I thought ahead."

"I didn't think a gun?" Laurie says.

"What did you think we we're gonna ward-off killers with, a tree-stick?" Harry says in jest. "Look," Harry says, "it's just for precautionary measures. You can't be too careful out here." Harry puts down the gun and reaches back into the bag. He pulls out twenty FN 5.7x28mm cartridges, the contents of a standard magazine. He puts those next to the gun. Reaching back into the bag again, Harry says, "And this is for you, Brian." He pulls out an all-black Glock 44 .22 LR caliber pistol and hands it to Brian.

"Oh man," Brian says excitedly.

"Oh jeez," Sarah says, "he is in heaven now." Brian cautiously rotates the gun with both hands in observance.

"Where did you get these from?" Brian asks.

"I know people," Harry responded.

"Are they legal?" Sarah asked.

"This is the wild west, everything is legal out here," Harry said with a smile.

"I'll take that as a, no," Sarah retorted. Harry puts the guns and ammunition back in the bag.

"Oh, I almost forgot," Harry says. He reaches back into the bag and pulls out a bag filled with white powder.

"I got this from the guy I bought the guns from," Harry says.

"Man, we haven't done that since college," Brian says.

"It's going to be one of those nights alright," Sarah mentions.

"We've been drinking all day and this will give us just the boost we need," Harry explains.

"How much you got?" asked Brian.

"An eight-ball of pure Venezuelan fiya!" said Harry. Sarah looked over at Laurie, who did not look as excited as the others.

"Have you ever?" asked Sarah.

"Oh, no. But you guys have at it."

Harry grabs a credit card and uses it to scoop out a large amount of the powder. He grabs the mirror hanging on the wall and lays it down on the table. He uses the credit card to chop the small rocks into a finely-ground powder. He separates the powder into four big lines.

Brian is up first. Brian leans over, holds his right-nostril closed and—with the straw in his left-nostril and dangling the straw just above one of the white lines—he snorts up. The line disappears quickly into his nose. "Woo," Brian shouts, sounding like Rick Flair. He crunches his face and closes his eyes as he hands the straw to Sarah. She repeats the process, but snorted it up with her right-nostril. Harry grabs the straw and spreads his feet, giving himself a wide base. Harry snorts it up with ferocity, making a loud snorting sound. They all look at Laurie. Sarah grabs the straw and reaches it out to her. Sarah makes a soft gesture to Laurie, giving Laurie the option without pressure or judgement.

"What the hell," Laurie says. Everyone cheers.

"Okay, so you grab the straw and hold one nostril closed," said Harry. "Don't be afraid, just get it up there good." Laurie snorts the line up like a pro, and the group again cheers her. Laurie had now officially become one of them. Harry then says to Laurie, "Cue the music maestro."

Laurie grabs the blue tooth speaker and plays the music through her phone. She opens her music app and puts on the song, *Beast of Burden*, by *The Rolling Stones*. Harry, again, shows more of his enigmatic dance moves. Laurie starts dancing seductively, with her hands above her head and swerving like a snake. Brian and Sarah also start dancing. The females have a smooth, rhythmic, seductive flow to their dancing. The men are all over the place. No rhythm, and puzzling dance moves.

Brian starts doing the Beavis dance, thrusting his hips back and forth and smacking the air, as if he was smacking a woman's backside. Harry, on the other hand—although his dancing would be categorized as terrible—was somehow able to make it look funny and cool. Much like with anything that Harry does; when he is in a room his presence is big. He is dripping with charisma.

The song ends and another begins to play.

"Who is this?" Sarah asks.

"This is one of my favorite songs," says Laurie. "This is *Pain is Like My Friend* by indi artist, *Will Careed*."

"Wow, this is awesome," says Brian.

"Yeah, what a flow to it," Harry says.

Chapter 5

Camp Fire Light

Later that night, the crew took the party outside. They decided that the backyard would be the perfect place to end the evening. There was an inground pool with multicolored, ambient, LED, underwater pool lights that provided a majestic feel. Only a few feet away was a large circular concrete area with a brick firepit in the middle. With a look befitting harbor towns, lighthouses and sandy beaches; lay a 12-piece set perfect for open-air entertaining. The set contained six classic Adirondack chairs. Spaced conveniently in between them were three classic-looking side tables. Made with marine-grade lumber, the chairs have the look of natural wood.

Harry put himself in charge of lighting the fire. Laurie was in charge of the music. Brian took care of the alcohol. And Sarah oversaw everything, much like a supervisor. It had rained the night before, so Harry was having a hard time trying to keep a fire going.

"Harry, you alright over there?" Sarah asks. "Maybe you should do some extra kindling and build a tepee with the wood."

"I have a great trick," said Harry. "Give me a second." Harry rushes off. He heads through the double-glass doors and onto the checker-board marble floor. Sarah lights up a cigarette. She is seated in the chair around the fire pit, facing the double-glass doors. Laurie is sitting next to her, separated by a side table. Brian is at the tiki bar, right by the pool, mixing drinks.

"So, you and Harry are getting serious I see?" Says Sarah.

"He is a bit crazy, but he is a real softy underneath." Says Laurie. "I think we understand each other well in just a short time. It kind of just flows with us, without much effort. It's hard to explain."

"No, I understand. And I see it with you guys. He is a great guy. I've always said, he just needs to find a good woman to settle down with. Lord knows I've met some, shall we say, strange ones through him." Both women chuckled.

"I'm sure," Laurie says.

"But you are very different, so I'm glad for you both," Sarah mentions.

"I got it!" Harry shouts, as he re-enters abruptly through the glass doors, holding up a plastic bottle.

"What's that?" asked Brian.

"It's Crisco oil. It's an old trick I learned in the army."

"You weren't even in the army," Brian responds.

"You know what I mean, jerk off," Harry says, annoyed.

"You're going to put CRISCO onto the

fire?" Sarah said in an elevated tone.

"Just, just, just sit back and watch MacGyver at work."

"Wow," Brian said, "you are dating yourself with that reference."

Harry poured the oil all over the wood, sprayed some lighter fluid on top, and lit a piece of cardboard on fire. Once lit, he tossed the cardboard onto the wood. The fire lit quickly, and the flames with it. However, huge clouds of thick smoke engulfed the area. Sarah and Laurie jumped up and quickly moved away. Harry forged forward, with his head turned away from the pit, trying to ensure that the fire remained ablaze. He poked at the wood with the fire pit tongs and sprayed more lighter fluid on top.

"Harry, you're gonna burn down the mansion before you even spend one night in it," Sarah scoffed. Laurie and Brian just laughed.

"That's great," said Laurie, as she smiled. The heavy smoke soon subsided. The fire burned bright.

"See, MacGyver," Harry said gloatingly.

"That's really cool, Harry," Laurie said.

"You see, the oil burns really hot. So, it offsets the dampness of the wood." Harry always enjoyed showing off to women. He always stopped just short of pontification, though—which made it seem charming.

Brian passed out drinks to everyone. Laurie had the music playing low. All four were now seated. The fire was raging. Harry put the metal cover on top of the firepit and sat back. His back was facing the glass doors. Brian had settled in next to his wife, on her right side. Limber Laurie folded her right foot and rested it on the chair, with her left leg on top of her foot.

"Brian," Harry said, "remember when we used to play monopoly when we were kids?" Brian took another sip of his drink.

"Yeah. And you always had to be the banker so you could five-finger some extra cash," Brian said. Sarah and Laurie shared a laugh.

"I never cheated!" Harry exclaimed.

"Yeah okay," Brian said sarcastically. "You always wound up with more money than you should have had. Very shady."

"I think you are missing the point," Harry said. "This time we are on the same team. And we will be playing Monopoly for real. We take Boardwalk and Park Place and every other property. We own them all."

"I just think that there are too many variables here, Harry."

"Look," Harry said, "you know my parents have always looked down on me. Sure, I have money, but I need to create a legacy; something that I create on my own. I could never make my father proud, no matter how hard I tried. And my mother thinks I'm just a clown. Ever since my father died my whole perspective has changed. And now that I met Laurie it's changed me. I want to settle down. I want a family. I want my son or daughter to be proud of me. Not just because I was handed a lot of money, but because I made something of it."

"Aww, that's really nice, Harry," said Sarah. "I mean, you didn't have to buy a whole town that is abandoned because of toxic waste. You could have started a little bit more conservative. But it is what it is, and Brian would be happy to at least look at it and see what he can do for you." Sarah nudges Brian.

"Let's just take it one step at a time, Harry," Brian said reluctantly. Brian was always the one to bring Harry back down to reality. Their relationship was very well-balanced. Not necessarily the odd couple, though. Brian and Harry were very similar in many ways. But Brian knew how to stay level-headed. Harry was always in the clouds. Thinking big. But he never ever came down. Only Brian had the ability to keep Harry somewhat in check. On the other hand, it was Harry who had the ability to make Brian take chances that he wouldn't normally take. Like the time when Harry basically forced Brian to go out partying. Brian and Harry were college roommates. It was a Friday night. They both had a big test on Monday. Harry wanted to go to the big fraternity party. It was mid-year and undoubtedly the second-best party of the year, next to the end of the year party. Brian had dug in. He stood firm against Harry. But Harry was relentless. And finally, Brian folded.

At the party, Brian saw the beautiful

blonde woman that he had been eyeing since the year started. However, he never had the nerve to speak to her. All the men were chasing her, and Brian was intimidated. It was Harry who forced him to approach her, by snapping jabs at his testicles until he decided to go speak to her. The two almost came to fisticuffs over the incident, but Harry, again, was relentless. Brian was always bigger and stronger than Harry. Although, he would never hurt him. They were brothers since second grade. They did get into one bad fist-fight back in fifth grade, but that only made their friendship stronger. So, Brian did approach the woman that night. And he's been married to her for seven-years.

"How did you guys meet?" Laurie asks the couple.

"We met at a college fraternity party," Sarah said.

"Yeah," said Brian, "and the first thing she asked me was about Harry."

"What?" Laurie asks, shocked.

"She had been eyeing Harry all year," Brian said. Harry shrugged his shoulders and took a sip of his drink.

"That was a long, long time ago," Sarah explained. "And once I found out what kind of player Harry was, I realized I had made the right choice. Brian is everything I ever wanted; I just didn't know it right away. I was young."

"That's cause all the ladies always love the bad boy," Harry said mockingly. Sarah sent him a jeering smile.

"Once I realized he was retarded, I just felt sorry for him," Sarah said.

"Ohhhhh, that's just wrong, Sarah," said Harry.

"So, Laurie, we never discussed this. I'm very interested about your career," Brian commented. "Harry tells me you are an animal caretaker." Harry rolls his eyes.

"Oh, here we go. Do we have to talk about work now?" Harry said. He was not pleased.

"No, it's okay Harry," Laurie said politely.

"I just want to get to know her better," Brian responded.

"I am an animal caretaker. Basically, we feed, water, bath, groom, and exercise animals on the one hand. On the scientific side, we record their conditions, and report any problems, and answer questions about behavior, habitat, breeding habits, or activities. I went to Michigan State University. I received my Bachelor's degree in Animal Science. Basically, it focuses heavily on biology. I started out working for a vet. And just saved my money. When I had enough, I started my own business caretaking."

"Wow, that's really cool," Sarah said. "You must really love animals?" She asked.

"I do. I feel like I have a special connection with them. They are so innocent and devoid of all the nonsense that people bring."

"So, you are 1099?" Brian asked.

"I started as 1099, but I started an LLC. I currently have six employees. The company is called 'Fur Care.' Our moto is 'A hug, no more bugs, and a pet you will love.'"

"Girl, I gotta give you mad props," Sarah says. "You really carved out a nice living for yourself. And to do something you love and are passionate about is not really work, it's a lifestyle." Harry rolls his eyes and leans in.

"Oh God, a lifestyle?" Harry says, annoyed. "Are we done with this love-fest yet? I'm getting bored and nauseous." Everyone at the same time says, "Shut up!" Harry leans back and slumps in his chair. He grabs his drink, takes a big swig and lights a cigarette.

"What about you guys?" Laurie asks. "I know you are a prosecutor [Sarah] and you [Brian] an environmental engineer. What colleges did you go to?"

"Brian went to Harvard and I went to Yale," Sarah mentioned.

"Wow, that's pretty cool," said Laurie.

"Yeah, we are products of wealthy families," Sarah explained. "We know how privileged we have been. But believe me, we respect the struggle. Especially those who came from little and made something out of themselves."

"True, but you guys still worked very hard to get where you are. And you don't look down on people. I can see that in you guys."

"Well, I went to community college,

and dropped out after a year," said Harry. "I didn't feel as though college was for me. Except for the partying, of course."

"You were at more colleges than any of the students, Harry," Brian says with a huge smile, referring to Harry partying at several colleges.

"Yeah, luckily I had friends in all the best party schools." Harry always knew how to break the monotony with his cherubic nature. But they were genuinely interested in Laurie. Yet, Harry was relentless.

"Here." He said. Harry took out the bag of cocaine. He put a key inside the bag and scooped out a big chunk. "Make a fist and face your palm to the ground," Harry said. "I will put this on top of your hand." Harry drops the cocaine contents on top of Laurie's hand, between her index finger and thumb. "Now put it to your nose slowly and snort it up really fast," Harry directed. After she did so, Harry said, "That's called a bump."

"She's a regular pro," Sarah said. Harry then gave the others the same, and then did one himself.

"Sarah, what was your most

memorable case?" Laurie asked. Sarah looked up and to the left for a moment, as if in deep remembered thought.

"There have been so many. But I would say it would have to be..." Just then, both Sarah and Brian said at the same time, "...*The Clark case.*"

"It was big news," Brian said, proudly. "It went all the way to the Supreme Court." Laurie appears surprised.

"I represented a 3-year-old boy who had told his daycare teacher that his mother's boyfriend had physically abused her." Laurie put her left hand on her chest. Her mouth in a circle. Her heartbeat quickened. "Well," Sarah continued, "the boy was deemed too young to testify. However, the judge still allowed his comment identifying the mother's boyfriend to his teacher to be used at trial. He was found guilty of child abuse, but later, the Arizona Supreme Court ruled that the boy's statements were not admissible because the defendant had the constitutional right of cross-examination. Well there was no way I was letting this fucker get away! So, I appealed the decision to the Supreme Court of the United States and they overturned the decision, thankfully."

A tear ran down Laurie's cheek. "Oh my God, I actually read about that case and I was overwhelmed. I can't believe that was you." Laurie now had even more respect for Sarah. She would look at her different from that moment on. "You actually really made a difference in this world, I must say," Laurie stated. "You made it easier to try abuse cases with minors without forcing kids to testify!"

"Yeah, I mean, aside from just being in the right place at the right time, and just doing what anyone else in my position would do; I was abused myself as a child— by my uncle. So that case was very personal to me."

"I was abused as well," Laurie stated. "Also, by an uncle." Laurie's surprised look was now transferred to Sarah. "I will never forget, one day I tried to run away from him and he ran after me. And just when I almost made it to the door, he grabbed my shoulder and pulled me back. He threw me on the ground and started choking me. He made me promise never to tell or he said he would kill me and my mother. I was so scared that I never said a word." Tears began flowing from Laurie's eyes. Sarah moved her chair over next to Laurie and put her hand on her leg. "At his funereal," Laurie continued, "I was crying hysterically. I remember my mother saying, 'you must have really loved your uncle.' But she didn't know that I was reliving the moments of each terrifying encounter with him."

Laurie broke down in tears. Sarah pulled her to her feet and held her tightly. Both cried profusely. The two women were now officially bonded forever. "I'm sorry to bring the party down. That story just brought it all back for me," Laurie announced to the group.

"No," said Brian. "Please don't feel bad at all. I couldn't imagine. I'm sick thinking about it."

"I just wish the guy was still alive," Harry said, "so, I can go pay him a visit." Laurie wiped the tears from her eyes, and quickly regained her composure. The tension in the air had thickened. The others waiting silently; for what felt like minutes, but was only seconds.

"Maybe we should call it a night guys?" Sarah suggested.

"Yeah," Brian said, "it's getting late anyway, and we have a long day tomorrow."

The moment was ripe for the classic save by Harry. He did not function well in emotional or tension-filled situation. He always found a way to bring in a change of subject. And sometimes he even did so when it was proper.

"So, guys," Harry said, "we are headed to Pavoso tomorrow, and I rented a helicopter to take us there." Everyone stopped what they were doing and turned their attention toward Harry.

"You what?" Brian asked.

"Well, it's a long drive, and we're probably going to be in bad shape tomorrow, after all the boozing and stuff. So, I figured we can sleep in late, and then hop on the chopper. It's like a 30-minute ride by helicopter." By now, Sarah had her arm around Laurie, who had her head on Sarah's shoulder. She popped her head up.

"Well, that sounds like fun." Laurie

said. The crew headed back toward the house and retired to their rooms at that time, which was just after midnight.

Chapter 6

Trip to Pavoso

Morning always seems to come much too quickly when you've had too much to drink the night before. Plus, it was a fun, but strenuous day on their bodies. The flight in, the unpacking, the drinking, the cocaine, and the emotional ending to the evening; all had made for an unpleasant awakening.

Sarah was the first to wake up. She quietly slipped out of bed, as not to wake Brian. She headed downstairs to the kitchen where she had hoped to fix a pot of coffee. She poked around the kitchen looking for the combination of items that would make for a suitable pot of coffee, not knowing what she would find. The coffee maker was there on the counter. She searched through a few draws and cabinets until she found the coffee grinds. She was also able to find sugar and powdered coffee creamer. Unable to locate the paper filters; she made due with paper towels.

Within minutes the kitchen filled with the pleasant aroma of fresh, hot coffee. She opened the refrigerator to see if anything was salvageable. Yet, there was nothing inside. She closed the refrigerator and jumped back and let out a loud scream. Standing there was Harry.

"Don't do that!" She shouted. "You almost gave me a heart attack." Both Harry's face and shoulders were slumped low. His eyes half opened.

"Hey," he said, in a dull, monotone voice. He lifted his nose and took two sniffs. "Please tell me that's coffee I smell?"

"Jeez, you look like crap," Sarah said.

"I feel worse than I look," Harry responded. At that moment a loud sneeze could be heard just beyond the kitchen entrance. A moment later Brian walks through the entrance, in view of Harry and

Sarah. Brian takes a quick breath in, feels an invisible tickle in his nose, pauses for a moment, and then lets out another monstrous sneeze.

"God bless you," his wife says. "Are you okay?"

Brian tries to take a breath through his nostrils, but the congestion is blocking his airway.

"Here, blow your nose." Sarah hands him a paper towel.

"I'm never doing that stuff again!" Brian proclaims. "I'm too old for this shit."

"Where's Laurie," Sarah asked Harry.

"I'm right here," Laurie says. Laurie lets out a groan. "I feel like I got hit by a truck," she says.

"Have some coffee, hun," said Sarah, "you'll feel better." Sarah pours coffee for everyone.

"How the hell did you make coffee so fast?" said Brian.

"Magic!" Sarah said facetiously (as she wiggled her fingers, mimicking a magician).

"I have a massive headache," Laurie shares.

"You know what you need?" Harry says. "The hair of the dog that bit you: another drink."

"Are you nuts?" Laurie shouts.

"What's the plan?" Brian asks.

"We are going to meet the pilot on the helipad in an hour-and-a-half," Harry answers.

"Where is the helipad," asks Sarah.

"It's behind the tennis courts," Harry responds.

"There's a helipad on the property?" Laurie asks. "Who are you the president?" she says in jest. Rarely does Harry miss a chance to return with a witty comment. But he hadn't even taken a sip of his coffee yet, and his mind was elsewhere.

The group grabbed their coffees and sluggishly rushed to take showers and pack. Since there was no running water or electricity where they were going, they knew they had one last opportunity to shower for the next 24-hours or so. After their mad-dashes to shower, they gathered their things and headed to the helipad for their one-night adventure. The helicopter was waiting there once the group arrived. A lone man awaited them. Leaning with his right hand on the chopper and legs fold, was the pilot.

"Howdy y'all," the pilot says loudly.

"Oh, boy, someone's chipper this morning," Brian said unenthusiastically.

"Hey," Harry said, as he shook the pilot's hand. "I'm Harry, this is Sarah, Brian, and Laurie."

"I'm Chuck, but my friends call me Dizzy."

The group was shocked that the pilot was a White, blonde-haired male with a southern United States accent.

"We are all set to go," Harry says.

"Well, where are yer dowgs?" Dizzy asked.

"Are what?" Harry asked, confused.

"Yer dowgs."

"We don't have any," Sarah answers.

"You can't be going down to Pavoso without dowgs. Haven't you heard?" Dizzy exclaimed.

"Well, we don't have any, and we need to get down there. So, are you taking us or not?" Harry said. Harry could get quite snippy the morning after a good party.

"Well, I reckon I'm not going to be able to accommodate you folks. I'm not leading more people to their doom." Harry grabs Dizzy's arm and pulls him to the side. "Look, we need to get to Pavoso. This is a once in a lifetime chance and I'm not letting anything stop me, okay? I will give you an extra thousand dollars." Harry pulls out a wad of hundred dollar bills out of his bag and counts out ten of them. He hands them to Dizzy.

"Okay, right this way folks," says Dizzy. He turns to Harry and says in a low voice, "It's your funeral."

The helicopter is a Eurocopter Mercedes-Benz EC 145. A grand, luxurious piece of machinery. It has all of the luxuries of a famous German sports car, and can fly 153 mph at 17,000 feet above the ground. The chopper is roomy. The twin-engine aircraft and can carry up to nine passengers along with two crew members.

The group all entered the helicopter and strapped into their seats. Within minutes the chopper was in the air.

"What was that all about, Harry?"

Laurie asked.

"I'm not sure," he said. "This is getting weirder by the moment." Harry grabbed the two-way radio, designed to speak to the pilot while flying. He was determined to get answers.

"Dizzy."

"Is everything alright back there? What can I do ya for?"

"Tell us why you think we need dogs to go to Pavoso?" Harry asked. "You don't seem to be from around here. What's the deal?"

"I'm not from around here. Been here 10 years. Moved here from my hometown of Kentucky. My father had a farm and the farm life just wasn't for me. Always wanted to be a pilot, and always been sweet on choppers. So, I came down here, got a job flying with a company for a few years. Saved up enough money and started this business with my partner, Fernando, the guy you spoke with on the phone and made these reservations.

So, I'm going about my business one day, and this guy calls asking to take him and his wife to Pavoso for one night. This was almost a year to the day. Says he has some investment opportunity or something. So, I tell my partner, Fernando, and he tells me that we don't make trips there unless the people have dowgs. Well, that sounded bout the dumbest thing I ever heard. Bout rattled my brain around like a BB in a boxcar. So, I asked him why? He told me that about fifty or so years ago some little kid killed his father. They said his heart was a thumpin' gizzard. And the kid gutted his father like a pig. Then the kid's grandfather, who was of Aztec decent, beat the kid real good with a whip and exiled him from the property, giving him a bone from his father's body to carry in a bag as he left. But before doing so, the grandfather put some kind of curse on the kid, but that something went wrong during the spell, like the grandfather messed it up or something.

Anyway, legend has it that the kid walked and walked, far into the woods, where he was attacked and killed by a bunch of wild dowgs. To make matters worse, that night his mother and grandfather were found murdered and gutless in the cabin. A few years later some claimed they had seen the kid wandering around by the old coal mine. But then something stranger started happening. People started hearing this whistling sound. But it sounded like that old Aztec death whistle. I don't know if any of y'all ever heard that, but it's mighty scary. Sounds more like a scream. Anyhow, people started going missing. And they found a few of these missing people. But each was gutted, and a bone was missing from each of the bodies.

Now they say he roams Pavoso killing anyone he encounters. They say if the whistling sounds like it's close, it's actually far away, and you have time to run. And you better run faster than green grass through a goose. Cause that thing will slap ya to sleep and slap ya for sleeping. But if the whistling sounds like it's far away, he is close, and you're shit outta luck. They say he's slicker'n owl shit, and he's meaner than a wet panther. And they say he's uglier than a mud fence and he smells bad enough to gag a maggot too. And because the kid was killed by dowgs, they say he is afraid of them, and will not attack those who have them. A whip is also helpful, they say, because the grandfather whipped him real bad. They call him 'The Whistling Man,' because they say he has this menacing whistle that people hear right before he kills them. Oh, and of course, he is said to be possessed by some evil Aztec deity.

So, naturally, I thought this to be as ridiculous as a horseshoe on a hornet. So, I took the couple down there. Real nice couple too. Wanted me to pick them up in two days. They had no dowg, but managed to grab a whip at a gift shop before take-off, just for shits and giggles. Well, I went back two days later. I waited there for hours. But just before dark, I got my ass the hell outta there. They're still missing to this day. I can remember giving their descriptions to the cuerpo [police] like it was yesterday. The man had on a navy-blue zippered hoodie with chocolate brown cargo pants. You know, the ones with all them pockets on the sides. His wife had on blue jeans, long black boots, and one of those jackets with the fur on the hood. I don't think she knew what she was in for, dressing like that.

And Fernando's knickers are still in a knot over it. So, you people better come back safe! I don't know what to believe, but I've heard enough stories to know to steer clear of there. That's why I didn't wanna send y'all down there with one oar in the water."

"Very interesting, Dizzy. Thanks for the heads-up. How much longer until we arrive?" Harry asks.

"About another fifteen minutes," Dizzy responds.

"Okay, thanks."

"Over'n out."

Harry looks at the others, who are a mix between confused and amused.

"That beats an inflight movie any day," said Sarah. The group laughs.

"Well, I still think we ought to check the area for dissidents, regardless," Laurie urges the group.

"Your destination is just over these hills," Dizzy announces to the group. They all look out the windows at the magnificent view and high, rocky hills just ahead.

Moments later, the helicopter begins slowly vacillating to the left and to the right. The group looked around, in disarray. The tail shifted the craft, awkwardly. Then it leveled off.

"What the hell was that?" Brian shouted. Moments later the helicopter again began vacillating, this time even faster. Harry grabbed the CB Radio.

"Dizzy, what's going on up there," Harry asked in a troubled voice.

"We hit some pretty thick, dense fog. Visibility is very low. Nothing to worry about." By now, a bit of turbulence had set in. The craft shook and shifted. The passengers felt as though they were in a car going very fast on an extremely bumpy road.

"Strap in tight," Dizzy said.

The helicopter climbed to an altitude of 1,400 feet (430 m), from 1,300 feet. A thick fog had completely surrounded the aircraft, making it impossible for Dizzy to see. Suddenly, the helicopter began falling. It hurtled toward the ground at an unusually fast rate. The women started screaming as the chopper went into an increasing tail spin. Harry closed his eyes and braced for the worst. Brian yelled, "Oh God, not like this!"

The aircraft's warning system alerted Dizzy that it was getting too close to the ground. The helicopter ascended to an altitude of 800 feet (240 m) above mean sea level. Dizzy couldn't believe that he had mismanaged the fog so badly. He was by no means a novice. Flying was his life. He had all the best qualifications. Dizzy was a licensed commercial helicopter pilot, a certified flight instructor, and an instrument-certified pilot (which means he was certified to fly in clouds, rain, and *fog*). He had done this a million times without incident. However, it's times like these that test even the best in their field.

Seconds felt like hours. Dizzy tried desperately to regain control of the aircraft. Just when all had seemed lost to Dizzy, the helicopter inadvertently came out of the thick clouds. Visibility had returned. Dizzy had barely regained his bearings when he noticed that the chopper was quickly heading directly toward the mountain ridge. A certain fiery death was only moments away. Dizzy reacted swiftly, grabbing the collective pitch control lever in his left hand and pulling it up. This changed the pitch angle of the main rotor blades, causing the aircraft to pitch up sharply. He did this while simultaneously using the throttle to reduce speed, or turning that same pitch control lever to the right. He did this so suddenly that the aircraft immediately began yawing to the right and rolling right.

He quickly countered this effect by taking the cyclic pitch control lever with his right hand and gently maneuvering it to the left, which stopped the yawing. With his adrenaline flowing and quick moves to be made, in a split second; he knew that if he jerked the cyclic pitch control lever to the left too quickly it would cause the aircraft to rotate irreversible to that side, causing them to spin perilously to their deaths. Dizzy braced himself for impact, as he held the controls steady. There was nothing more he could do. The fate of the group was now in God's hands.

It was a close call. Too close!

Dizzy had managed to regain control of the helicopter without a second to spare, just missing the ridge by a few feet. The helicopter brusquely leveled off and was back to flying normal. It had all happened so fast.

"Holy shit," Brian screamed. "Did we just almost die?" They could not see much during the whole ordeal, but they did witness the helicopter coming dangerously close to the mountain ridge before pulling up.

"Are you guys okay back there?" Dizzy asked.

"What the fuck just happened, Dizzy?" Harry bellowed.

"That fog was pitching a hissy fit with a tail on it," Dizzy relayed. "I didn't know whether to check my ass for the time or scratch my watch! But no worries. All's well that ends well, and we're coming up on our final destination."

Minutes later the helicopter touched down in a large field, just past a wooded area. Dizzy opened up the doors, and one by one the group exited the chopper. Harry—in his usual dramatic fashion— jumped out, fell to his knees and kissed the ground. Sarah and Laurie held hands as they exited, frightened and relieved at the same time. Brian exited last. He seemed a bit more disheveled than the others. His first two steps were a bit wobbly. He walked over to Sarah and Laurie.

"No wonder why they call him Dizzy," he said.

"Sorry about that guys and gals," Dizzy said, "that was an uncommon occurrence. I was as confused as a fart in a wind factory for a second there."

"Well, let's just make sure you get that corrected for the ride home, okay?" Harry declared. "I didn't bring any diapers with me."

"Will do," said Dizzy. "I will be here at noon tomorrow, so please be here at that time. I won't wait more than an hour, ya hear?" The group said nothing. They were still gathering themselves and checking to be sure that they had all of their belongings.

"And remember what I said," Dizzy reminded them, "you see anything out of the ordinary, and I mean anything, you run like a cat in a room full of rocking chairs, now ya hear?"

"Cat in a room full of rocking chairs, got it," said Harry, facetiously.

"We'll see you tomorrow," Brian shouted, as they walked away from the helicopter.

"Oh," Dizzy shouted, "don't bother trying to use your cell phones up here. There's not a cell tower for miles." Laurie took out her cell phone and saw she had no signal bars.

"damn it," she cried.

"It's just one night," said Harry. "It'll be fine." Dizzy stood there for a moment, watching the group walk away. His hands nestled on his hips. Eyes squinted. A toothpick hanging out the side of his mouth.

"Those four are about as useful as a trap door on a canoe," Dizzy says to himself, while shaking his head side to side.

The roar of the helicopter engines starting were heard moments later. The group looked back to see Dizzy peel off into the sunlight, solidifying that they were truly stuck there for the night.

"Ah, is that an owl in that tree over there?" asked Sarah.

"Well look at that," says Harry. "He's here to great us."

"That sure is," Brian says.

"Those things are pretty scary," Harry says.

"That's a great horned owl, actually," Laurie explains. That is the most dangerous, deadly type of owl. It is about two-feet in length, and its wingspan is about 80 inches."

"Will it attack us?" Sarah asked anxiously.

"They have been known to attack humans, but usually only to protect their young or their territory. But just in case it does you should know that when they attack larger prey they concentrate on the face and head during the battle. They are quite efficient predators."

"Great, good to know. Very comforting Laurie," Sarah says in a sarcastic, worried tone. The owl watched the group closely as they walked through town.

Then, it let out a loud screeching, shrieking sound that made Sarah jump, and then flew off.

"Friggen creepy," said Sarah.

Chapter 7

The Abandoned Town of Pavoso

The small town of Pavoso is approximately .097 square miles, making it one of the smallest towns in the world. It is surrounded on all sides by a condensed forest leading to mountains. There is a small river that runs through the eastern corridor of the town. The town only has access to a very small portion of the river, which is used as a docking area. It is one of only two ways out of the town. The river leads to a town nearby, through the only break in the surrounding mountain. The other way out is by helicopter. Of course, a climb over the steep, high mountains is a third option, but not very practical for humans.

Pine trees not only make up the surrounding forest; they are also scattered throughout the town. The roads in the town are made up of dirt and gravel. The pedestrians of the town were not allowed to have vehicles. However, prior to its vacancy, the town offered two mini vans that chartered residents to any location within town. The mini vans traveled every hour as needed, and did this usual route from 7am to 6pm.

The western-most part of town was filled by farm land. The town made most, if not all, of its money from the agricultural products that were produced there. The farm has the capability of producing a unique variety of consumer products including rice, corn, cotton, and its two most valuable and profitable commodities: tobacco and coffee. Seventy-five to eighty percent of the adults living in the town, prior to its collapse, worked for the farm in some capacity.

The cabin, where the group will be staying, is located just east of the farm, just off *Main Road*. The helicopter drop-site is next to the farm's north-west border. The mine is just past the farm's southern border.

Three roads run east and west in the town. All three lead to the farm. The northern most one of these roads is *Church Street*. Adequately titled, as it leads to the only church in town, which is located just east of the farm, near its northern border. Following Church Street going east; there you will find resident housing cabins all along the northeast side. On the right side of the road, just past the connecting *Route 9*, is the school/daycare center and the one and only convenience store. The hospital is a bit further down, on the eastern edge of the town. Main Road is the second of the three roads running east and west. It runs directly through the center of town. It passes by the cabin moving west and ends at the farm.

Moving east past the cabin; more resident housing is located before and after the intersecting Route 9. Just past Route 9, the school/day care and convenience stores are on the left. The mayor's office, police station and the municipal court are all located in the same building. This is located to the right of Main Road, near the end of the street. Just past that building, Main Road splits into three directions. Slight-right leads to *Doc Blvd.* This street is about 75 feet (22.86 m) long, extending to the northern side of the dock, which is essentially behind the police station. As mentioned, this is one of only two ways out of the town.

The middle split of Main Road is called *Café Lane.* This street is 70 feet (21.3 m) long, and the second hospital entrance is located on the left. The street ends just before the small woods that lead to the mountain. The third split of Main Road is by making a left turn onto *Hospital Way.* In doing so, the main hospital entrance Is located on the right and convenience store on the left. Hospital Way also leads to the housing section if you continue further north, just beyond the Church Street intersection.

The third and final street traveling

east and west is *Joggers Trail*. This street runs along the town's southern border. It extends from the mine (in the western section)—features housing before and after its Route 9 intersection—and runs around the back of the police station (in the eastern section), and ends at the southern entrance of the dock.

Three streets travel north and south in the town. Hospital way, as mentioned, is one. Also Route 9, which runs through the center of town and intersects with all three east/west moving streets. Route 9, past the Church Street intersection, leads to the final portion of housing on its eastern side. The final street running north and south is *Fisher Avenue*. Fisher runs from Church Street (ending just in front of the church) to Main Road.

The New Visitors

The group arrived in Pavoso on Wednesday, October 30, 2019; the day before Halloween in the United States. In Venezuela they do not celebrate Halloween. They do celebrate something similar, however. It's called 'The Day of the Dead,' but it's celebrated a few days later, on November 2nd.

From the Helipad they trekked forward through the high grass. The land, for the most part, looked surprisingly maintained. Although, the government had only partially maintained certain areas. This would now be Harry's job, to pay and schedule maintenance going forward. Harry had already spoken to and procured the current cleaning crew. He figured that they knew the area better than he did, so why not use them! They were also pretty cheap, comparatively. Harry didn't really look to far into other companies. For him, he figured, the less trivial stuff he had to deal with the better.

The group walked along the farm's fence, heading south-bound. Harry had two maps of the area. One was the old map, which showed the town as it once was. The other map he had made. It was basically the same, but Harry had named the streets in English in order to identify them easier.

"It's just around this bend guys," said Harry. They continued along the farm's fence for another hundred yards or so until they saw a lone cabin next to a road.

"Is that it over there?" Laurie asked.

"Yup, home, sweet home," Harry said.

The cabin had an extension put on it prior to the town being vacated. It went from being one of the smaller cabins in the town to the biggest. The family that lived there before was the last mayor of the town. However, he and his family went missing one night and were never found. This just added to the lore of the town and of The Whistling Man.

The fact that the family disappeared in the middle of the night certainly puzzled the residents. Many different reasons were postulated as to why this might have occurred. One, was that the mayor was under some political pressure. His approval rating in the town had dissipated significantly. Others say he just wanted out. So, they say he and his family boarded a vessel late at night and sailed far away. But the most pervasive rumor is that they were taken late at night by the whistling man. In any case, the group had no idea of this—or any of the history of the town, for that matter.

Harry only knew what he thought he needed to know in order to make money and restore the area. The group was excited to get to the cabin and get settled in. Passing over Main Road, the group came upon a short dirt path leading to the cabin's front door. The cabin was well maintained by the maintenance crew. It was used as the maintenance crew's main hub while working on the town.

"Wow," Laurie said, "this is really woodsy." She was not happy about the technological deficiencies that she would have to endure. No TV, no electricity, no cell phone (or any type of phone); this trip was not meant for the modern, spoiled American. No one was happy about it, in fact. But Harry's excitement for the project and having his buddy, Brian, to help was distracting him from the lack of modern *essentials*.

The group approached the house. They stood about twenty-yards away when they noticed something strange.

"*Caw, caw,*" sounded loudly.

About twenty crows were circling the house from above. They formed a large circle, as if in some coordinated sky-dance.

"I guess nature has truly taken over this place," said Harry.

"Ew," shouted Sarah, as she looked at her shoulder. "One of those fucking crows just shit on my new jacket!" She exclaimed. Brian started chuckling. "It's not funny, Brian!" Sarah said in anger.

"It's good luck," said Brian. Sarah was in no mood to hear that. She rolled her eyes and took her jacket off. By now, the group was only about five-yards from the house.

The door swings open. Laurie is standing in the doorway. Her head swivels and her eyes ricochet around the room like a pinball bouncing off of different targets.

"Wow, very cozy," Laurie says, as she enters. Harry walks in next, and then Sarah, followed by Brian.

Settling In

The cabin has an oblique shape. When viewing the home virtually from the air, it sits diagonal on its lot, like a desk that sits catty-corner in a room. The left side is the original home; however, it's been largely modified. The placement of the front door has not changed. The *now* hallway was once the living room. Looking left, what was once the kitchen is *now* the dining room. To the right of the hallway is a big kitchen, which is part of the extension. Past the kitchen is a bathroom and a large family room. The basement is small. It was mostly used as a storage area. That entrance is in the hallway to the left of the stairs, which leads to the second floor.

Upstairs is a small hallway leading to the second bedroom. Next to it, the master bedroom. There are two windows in the master bedroom. One faces the farm, at the back of the house. The second faces south. The second bedroom has one window facing the farm. Both bedrooms are part of the original construction.

Sarah tended to the kitchen. Brian worked with her as her aid. The group had packed several foods for their 24-hour stay. Sarah had volunteered her services to head this effort. She made a list of foods they would need, knowing that there was no electricity. On her list was low-sodium canned beans, canned vegetables, canned fruits, peanut butter and jelly, a loaf of bread, pouches of fully cooked whole grains, nuts, whole-wheat crackers, snack bars, and a few bags of chips. They also had a mini grill and a bag of charcoal. They packed a small cooler full of chopped meat, hotdogs, and chicken. Perhaps the most important things they had with them were two-cases of bottled water. Since there was no running water, these were quite possibly their most important items. One case would be for drinking. The other, for hand washing, and anything short of a shower. There was also plenty of firewood sitting near the fireplace.

Laurie walked up the stairs. She had an eerie feeling as she took the last few steps. 'Something was not right,' she thought. However, she tried to brush off the feeling and continued on. 'What else could she do?' she thought. She was stuck there, like the rest of them. Laurie was cautious of mind before anything else. It's not that she did not like to take risks. It's that she had been through a few traumas in her life, and she had finally had peace. Being an *adopted child* had a lot to do with her cautious nature. It wasn't that she wasn't tough. Quite the opposite. Yet, she was well aware of what could happen when a person invites trouble. The others, she believed, either never had such trauma or were more focused on other things. They felt more secure. Like nothing could hurt them. They had lived an entitled life up to that point. But Laurie knew that once your mortality is threatened or control is lost, a person becomes more conservative with the risks they take. 'Much like children believe that they are invincible,' she thought of the others. A certain naivety in this area accompanied them.

Laurie placed Harry's suitcase on the bed. There was a dresser in the room. It had four drawers (one on top of the other). She opened the case and began placing Harry's clothes in the top drawer. Once she was done with Harry's clothes, she removed his case from the bed and flopped her suitcase firmly on the bed. As she opened it, Harry walked in. Laurie looked back, then continued unpacking. Harry dropped the bag he was carrying by the door and headed toward her. He looked and saw that Laurie had emptied his other bag.

"Thanks for putting my clothes away, hun." Harry moved closer and hugged her from behind.

"Are you guys going to look around a bit and make sure that we are safe and alone?"

"Hun, there is no one here. This place is abandoned."

"You promised you were going to check, Harry."

"Yes, we will, babe. We are heading to the mine after lunch. I will make sure that we secure the area." Laurie stayed silent. The way Harry answered and the tone he used made her even more skeptical that he would handle the situation properly. She didn't think he was taking her suggestion seriously enough.

"Did you bring the candles?" Laurie asked. Harry turned and approached the bag he had put on the floor. Laurie was in front of the window, facing the back of the house. As she waited for Harry's response, something in the window inadvertently caught her eye. She looked up quickly. She saw someone standing in the back of the house, about 20 yards from the cabin. At first, she wasn't sure what she was looking at, even though the image was clear. Her eye site was 20/20, so the image was clearly distinguishable. She locked-in on it. The person stood firm, not moving, looking directly at her, in an empty field in the backyard. Now she was sure.

"Harry, come quick! Look!" She exclaimed. She pointed out the window. Harry walked over slowly, ignoring the urgency in her voice. Her eyes were locked on the image. The person stood as still as a big rock. She turned to look for Harry, as he was taking longer than her tone had required. Harry approached and looked out of the window over her shoulder.

"What?" he asked. Laurie turned back quickly.

"Right there," she said, then quickly paused. "Wait," she cried. "He was right there!" she shouted. All's Harry saw was a few crows flying around.

"Who was where?" Harry asked.

"There was a person standing right

there," her hand, shaking, but still pointing to the spot where she saw him. "Right there, where that owl is. He had a navy-blue hoodie with the hood on his head. He was looking up here, right at me." Laurie sounded adamant and her anxiousness was visible on her face.

"Laurie, you probably just thought that you saw something. You're just nervous after that Dizzy character told us that story. No one is here, but us."

"I'm telling you, Harry, someone was there. I'm not going crazy."

"Okay, Brian and I will go check it out. We are leaving soon to go to the mine anyway. We will sweep and secure the area."

Harry walked down the stairs and headed to the kitchen. Brian was putting the snow from outside on the meats in the cooler. Sarah was up on a step stool putting away cups, paper plates, canned foods, and snacks.

"Brian, are you ready to go?" Harry asked.

"Yeah, let's do this," said Brian.

"Look, Laurie is a bit weirded out,"

Harry said.

"Why, what's wrong?" asked Sarah.

"She thought she saw someone in a hoodie in the yard staring up at her," Harry responded.

"What?" Sarah asked. "Did you see it also?" Sarah asked again nervously.

"I looked, but there was no one there."

"She is probably just spooked about this trip after what we heard," Brian announced.

"I'm telling you, I saw someone out there," Laurie said, as she entered the kitchen.

"What did he look like?" asked Sarah.

"I couldn't see his face. He had a hood on, and it was covering his eyes."

"Maybe it was that guy who Dizzy said he brought down here and was never found," Sarah postulated.

"Brian and I are going to head to the mine now, so we will take a look around," said Harry.

"Yeah," said Brian, "we should go now so we are back by nightfall."

"If it's him, we can bring him back

here and back with us when we leave,"
Harry said.

"Hopefully his wife is okay as well,"
Sarah said.

Harry went over to the blue duffle
bag and took out both guns and two
flashlights. Harry holstered his FN Five-
sevenN USG handgun.

"You know how to use this thing?"
Harry asked Laurie.

"No, I've never fired a gun before,"
said Laurie.

"Sarah, show her how to use this
please," Harry suggested. "If anyone comes
here, for any reason, do not let them in
until we return," Brian demanded.

The boys walked out the front door
of the cabin and made a sharp right turn.
They headed toward the back of the cabin.
They moved south-west, as the mine was
located just beyond the southern-border of
the farm.

"How do those 5.7x28mm rounds
shoot?" Brian asked. "I've never shot one of
those before."

"Wanna try it?" Harry asked, as he
unholstered the weapon, flipped it (so that

he had hold of the barrel), and handed it to Brian. Brian took aim at a tree about 20 yards away. He fired a shot.

Bang!

The bullet hit the side of the tree, ripping off a small piece of dead bark.

"That's got some kick to it. Not as much force as the 9mm, but close," Brian stated.

"I prefer the .22 caliber, myself," Harry said. "I know it doesn't have the stopping power of the 9mm or the 5.7x28mm rounds, but it's just smoother and more accurate, in my opinion. Plus, I don't expect we will be getting into a firefight out here, so." The two laughed.

"That Laurie is something, man," Brian said. "She is great, but a little paranoid."

"Well, Brian, I kinda like that about her. Lord knows I can use a bit of conservatism to counteract my liberal ways."

"Ain't that the truth," Brian said, sarcastically.

More crows circled overhead, as the men continued walking along the dirt path. The owl that had greeted them earlier—and was standing in the yard during Laurie's alleged sighting—was now watching them from a nearby tree branch.

Chapter 8

Things are 'Heating Up'

Back at the cabin, Sarah had just finished stocking the kitchen with supplies, and Laurie had finished unpacking. The two had just reconvened in the living room. Laurie is still a bit shaken over the sighting of the stranger. She has been looking out the window periodically to see if she could spot the unwanted guest again. Sarah sits down on the couch and lets out a big sigh.

"Finally, I can relax a bit," Sarah says. "Would you like to open a bottle of wine, or should I?"

"Sure, go ahead," Laurie says. Sarah pops back up and heads toward the kitchen. Laurie walks over to the bag sitting on the ground near the front door.

"Hey Sarah, wasn't there another bag with candles that we had?" Sarah rushes back into the living.

"Oh Lord, we forgot the other bag!" Sarah exclaims.

"Maybe there are more candles in the basement," Laurie suggests.

"Couldn't hurt to try. We should go now. It will be dark before we know it."

The women head to the basement door. Laurie opens it and stops.

"It's pretty dark down there," she says.

"Hold on," said Sarah, "let me get some flash lights." Sarah reaches into the bag and pulls out the final two flashlights.

"Okay," Sarah says, as she hands one to Laurie. "Let's go."

Laurie leads the way, walking slowly down the old, creaky wooden stairs. There are no windows in the basement. If not for the flash lights the women would not be able to see at all. Laurie reaches the bottom of the stairs. She makes a left.

"I'll go this way and you look over there," Laurie says.

"What's that smell?" Sarah asks. She holds her nose closed in an effort to thwart the revolting smell.

"Smells like mold," Laurie says.

"Smells like secrets and body odor down here," Sarah replied.

"Well," Laurie continued, "it's a mix of volatile organic compounds, no light, and no ventilation. If you touch anything don't touch your face until we wash our hands."

"I'm not touching shit down here," Sarah said in disgust.

The musty, fetid odor was almost too much for Sarah to handle. The basement was crowded with old stuff. An inch of dust coated every item down there. Laurie came upon a large old contraption. She wondered what it was used for. It looked like some type of stove. None that she had ever seen, but it had a slight resemblance. She looked it over, flashing the light on every piece of it. She was fascinated. She looked on the side to see if she could find the word 'stove' or 'heater' on it. She bent down on the left side of it and saw a metal model and serial number imprinted on the side, 27-12-A (42891). 'The new owners must have replaced this oven when they moved in,' she thought.

Laurie was about to call Sarah over to see it, but before she could, a loud noise sounded. Several old pots fell off of the shelf near Sarah. Laurie turned quickly. Sarah let out a horrific scream.

"What is it, Sarah?" Laurie asked, in a concerned voice. Sarah had illuminated a mouse with her flashlight that had scurried under the stairs.

"That's it," Sarah shouted. "Fuck the candles."

"Wait!" Laurie insisted. "What's this?"

Laurie reached down and grabbed an old carrycase from the shelf. Sarah walked over to Laurie slowly, still keeping an eye out for that pesky mouse. Laurie blew a thick layer of dust off of the case. Sarah waved her hand in front of her face, as some of the dust had traveled her way.

"What is it?" Sarah said, uninterestedly.

"I don't know, but it definitely is something. Looks like some kind of reliquary or something." Laurie was very intrigued. There was an embroidered design on the outside of the case. An odd shaped bird with his wings spread, large feathered tail showing and his head facing to the left. She sat the case down on a small workbench nearby. There was a small keyhole in the middle of the case in between the two attached ends of the handle. Laurie pressed the two buttons on the side of the case simultaneously. The two case lock bars snapped open, making a definitely resounding *click*. She opened the case. Inside was a book, with the same symbol on the cover as on the case. There were also eight very small jars. Six of the jars contained a different colored powder inside each. Two of the jars contained black powder.

She opened the book cover, and on the inside of the book cover, the name *Zuma* was written. She browsed a few pages briefly.

"What is it?" Sarah asked again, this time inquisitively.

"It looks like an ancient Aztec book of spells," Laurie replied.

"The Aztecs?" Sarah said. She was now fully engaged. "You know, that is probably worth a lot of money if it's authentic."

At that moment, Sarah jumped as she heard a tiny scatter of footsteps. Both women turned and witnessed the mouse running across the other side of the basement floor. Sarah appeared spooked. As their heads were turned, the book mysteriously flipped ahead several pages, and then settled. What made it odd was that there had been no wind down there at all. Certainly, there was not a wind gust strong enough to turn several pages in a book. And definitely not as quickly and deliberately as this had been done. Nevertheless, the women never saw the pages turning. They were busy focusing on the mouse.

"Will you relax?" Laurie said. "It's just a mouse. It's more scared of you than you are of it."

"Those things carry disease," Sarah retorted. "I'm not used to sleeping with rodents. I will never sleep tonight!" Laurie turned back to the book.

"Check this out," she said. "This spell is for the Goddess, *'Toci,'* to enter your body and protect you from evil spirits. Apparently, Toci is the *mother of the gods.*" Laurie continues reading. She opens up the jar with the blue powder in it.

"What are you doing?" Sarah asked.

Laurie took a pinch of the powder and sprinkled it on her own head.

"I'm gonna try this spell out," Laurie said. "I wanted to be a witch when I was younger. This may be my last chance."

"I don't think you should be messing with that stuff," Sarah said, concerned.

"Oh. What's the worst that can happen?" Laurie said facetiously.

"I don't know," Sarah responded. "Maybe you turn into a goat or something. Or worse, a mouse!" Both women shared a laugh.

"Well, if I turn into a goat, make sure I get all the hay I can manage, ok?"

Laurie carefully closed the jar and steadily put it back in the case. She then grabbed the jar with the silver powder in it. She opened it and took a pinch and placed it on her head as well. She carefully put that jar back and grabbed the jar with the black powder in it.

"Why are there two jars with black and the rest only one color of each?" Sarah asked.

"I don't know," Laurie said. "I'm assuming black is probably used in more spells. Okay, it says here that I must flick the black powder over my left shoulder, then my right shoulder, and then my left shoulder again; all while chanting the phrases written here. It warns not to spill a drop of powder from my head until the spell is completed." Laurie steadies herself. "Here goes nothing."

Laurie flicked the black powder over her left shoulder.

"Pee-ahh-lee, Ah-wee-zo-tul." She grabbed another pinch of the black powder and flicked it over her right shoulder.

"Nee-meetz-tla-tlaw-ti-ah, Ah-wee-zo-tul." Once again, she grabbed the final pinch of the black powder. She pauses for a second and looks at Sarah, who shrugs her shoulders. Laurie flicks the black powder over her left shoulder a second time.

"Tlah-so-cah-mah-tee, Ah-wee-zo-tul."

Both women pause for a second, almost bracing themselves for a reaction.

"Well, that was fun," Sarah says. "What next; you gonna pull a bunny out of..."

BOOM!

At that moment, a loud blast, an explosion, rocks the basement. The shock waves jolt Sarah off her feet. The basement shakes. Sarah falls on her bottom, but her eyes still remain focused on Laurie. The shock wave appears very controlled. It only appears to affect the ambit surroundings of the women. Laurie is shaking violently. Her eyes look like balls of light. Sarah watches as the remnants of the blast contract and disappear into Laurie. Once this happens, Laurie's eyes roll to the top of her head, her eyelids close and she falls to the floor softly, as her body goes completely limp.

'Laurie!" she screams from her

seated position. Sarah springs up and runs to her aid. She cradles her from a kneeling position. "Laurie, Laurie!" Sarah screams frantically. Laurie opens her eyes. She is dazed.

"What the hell was that?" Laurie asked. Sarah laughs. Partly because Laurie's response was humorous, and partly because she was relived.

"It was some kind of earthquake or something," Sarah said in confusion. "Are you okay? Sarah asks. Laurie nods her head up and down. She is still a bit hazy. "Let's just go back upstairs," Sarah says. "I'm kneeling on a floor with mice droppings, ew."

Sarah helps Laurie to her feet. Laurie still appears a bit dazed, groggy. Sarah helps her up and holds Laurie's arm to ensure that she does not fall. Laurie is quickly regaining her equilibrium, but is still a bit woozy.

As they walk up the stairs, Laurie says, "Ya know, I just had the weirdest dream. I saw this beautiful woman, kinda like ghostly, floating in a white gown. She was, like, beckoning me. I was reluctant, but

I finally gave into her. Then, I saw you guys screaming in terror."

"You guys?" Sarah asks.

"Yeah, you, Brian and Harry," Laurie prognosticated.

"Well, you were knocked out," Sarah says. "The mind plays tricks. Let's get you some water."

Sarah sat Laurie down on a stool by the front door.

"Wait here. I will get you some water."

Laurie puts her hand on her head, trying to shake away the cobwebs. Laurie turns and looks out the glass window that is located directly to the left of the front door. She squints her eyes, as she thinks she sees someone. The figure had returned. There he stood, twenty-yards from the front door of the cabin. This time, however, he looked to be holding a large knife in his right hand, blade facing away from his body. She squinted and moved closer to the window to get a better look. Sarah hurried in with a bottle of water.

"What are you doing?" Sarah asked.

"Shh!" Laurie uttered loudly. "Come

quick!"

"Let me guess, the lady in the gown?" Sarah answered sarcastically.

The figure turned quickly and started running extremely fast.

"Hurry!" Laurie shouted. Sarah approached the glass, but it was too late. Laurie opened the door and started running after the figure.

"Hey, you!" she screamed, as she stopped about ten-yards in front of the cabin and lost sight of the figure. By now it was a good fifty-yards away. Sarah followed, and saw just a dash of something.

"Did you see that?" Laurie asked.

"I think so," she said confusedly.

"You just hit your head," said Sarah. "Your mind is playing tricks. You need to chill for a bit."

"He had a big knife, Sarah. I'm telling you. I saw it!"

"Well, let's just lock the door and keep a lookout until the men come back," Sarah suggested. "We do have a gun."

Laurie continued to look around for anything moving, but saw nothing except for an owl sitting on a tree branch in the area where she believed the perpetrator had gone. As the women turned and headed back inside, something was watching them from that very tree, some fifty-yards away.

Surveying the damage

By now the men had reached the mine. The mine sits in the side of the mountain. It's about a thirty-yard hike from the base of the mountain to the protruding, rotting, wooden mine entrance. As they approached the entrance, Brian stopped.

"You see those paw prints in the snow?" Brian asked.

"What the hell is that from?" Harry asked anxiously.

"That's from a bear. We need to be extremely careful."

"You're telling me a fucking bear lives in there and we are just going to walk in?" Harry questions.

"We have one night here," said Brian. "You wanna do this or not?"

Harry rolls his eyes and proceeds forward, reluctantly. A make-shift, wooden bridge is laid out as a walkway leading into the entrance of the mine. It's shaky, at best. Brian leads the way, heading over the wobbly structure.

"Watch your step," Brian says, as he moves slowly across. Underneath is a break in the ice and ground. A drop of twenty feet or more lies below, into a muddy abyss.

"The door won't open," Brian announces. "It's stuck." Harry notices a small crack in the wood that requires a short leap from the bridge.

"Through here," said Harry. He jumps and grabs a piece of wood with his right hand, unaware that it is not sturdy. The wood gives way, and he begins to fall backwards. Harry manages to grab onto the other side of the wooden entrance with his left hand just in time. He steadies himself and jumps through the hole.

"Jesus, that was close," Harry remarks. "Here, give me your hand," Harry says as reaches out. Without hesitation, Brian takes the leap. They clench their right hands together tightly, and Harry pulls Brian to safety. Once inside, they immediately notice a mine-railway that splits in two directions, and a mine cart lying on its side. Both were used for moving ore and materials procured in the process of traditional mining. A thick layer of ice coats the floor in most areas, as well as the ceilings. The wood that surrounds the area is rotting and unstable.

As they survey the area, they come across old fans and machinery used in the mining process. In most places the ground is mixed with ice and mud. In whatever direction they travel, it's extremely slippery. They come upon a room that looks like it was used by the workers as a room for taking breaks. They see gloves left from miners, empty canteens, old signs, empty and rotting coffee cans, and other abandoned materials. Harry takes comfort in the many pictures on the wall. Most of them unrecognizable, but some show beautiful, scantily clad Venezuelan women, there to lift the spirits and morale of the male workers.

The mine is much bigger than they had anticipated. There were numerous rooms. Along their expedition, they came upon two other entrances into the mine besides the one that they had entered from. There were also two areas to go down deeper into the mine, but both were blocked off by collapsed dirt and debris.

Brian collected numerous samples along the way. He also had a high-tech, hand-held machine that could test the toxicity levels of the water and dirt within the mine. Many areas of the mine saw the ground with large puddles of water. This was a result of warmer temperatures within the mine, causing the ice to melt. Around a winding corridor, they entered into another room.

"Thank God I brought another pair of sneakers," Harry said, as they marched through nearly a foot of water in one area. After about an hour and a half of exploration and testing, Brian came to a shocking conclusion.

"It appears that the overwhelming concentration of contamination came from the tailings of the beneficiation process, which occurred *AFTER* the mine was abandoned, and not from whatever they had originally believed it to be."

"Can you repeat that in English?"

Harry asks sarcastically.

"Okay, so, the purpose of mining is to find ores, that's O-R-E. An 'ore' is a naturally occurring solid material from which a metal or valuable mineral can be profitably extracted. Well, the question becomes, how does one extract the valuable mineral from the ores? They do this by beneficiation, or reducing it in size by crushing and/or grinding. There are waste products that result from this process, like mercury, copper sulfate, sodium cyanide, bad shit! It appears that they managed this process quite well and efficiently. However, the irony is; their contamination came from them abandoning the land and not the other way around."

"Are you fucking shitting me?"

"I shit you not, my friend. In fact, even better news is that the contamination currently is not that severe at all. It's a minor clean-up, separate from restoring the mine, of course."

Harry jumps up and throws his right fist in the air.

"YES!" he screams. "We're gonna be rich," harry sings. "We're gonna be rich."

"You already are rich, idiot."

"Richer, I mean."

"I still need to do a thorough sampling and an analysis plan, but from my experience I don't think anything else will turn up. My only real concern is if this place is not contaminated, like you said, why did people actually leave?"

"Who knows, man," Harry responded. "Maybe their little thinga-ma-jiggies like yours were more primitive. Whatever the case, it's time to celebrate. Let's head back to the cabin and tell the girls the good news."

Close Encounters

Brian turned and noticed another room that they hadn't ventured into yet.

"Hey, what's in here?" asked Brian. They noticed two small clay statues, one on each side of the entrance. The small statues stood only two feet high. Both were identical.

"What the hell are those?" Harry asked.

"Looks like some sort of depictions of

a skeleton with some weird headgear on," Brian responded. Brian took a few steps into the room and saw a bit of smoke emanating from a stack of branches that had been neatly stacked in the corner.

"Looks like someone's been here very recently," Brian said.

"Maybe it's that couple that Dizzy dropped off here," Harry said. Harry turned his flashlight to the wall.

"What the hell is this?" he said, sounding surprised. On the wall was a large picture of a skeleton head with its tongue sticking out. Surrounding it were two rings, a smaller one and a larger one, just like the two clay statues at the entrance.

"Looks like blood," Brian said.

"This is some creepy shit, bro," Harry claimed.

As Brian scoured the walls with his flashlight, he illuminated several more hand-painted figures, including spiders, bats, and mostly owls.

"If this is the guy Dizzy left here, I'm not sure I want to meet him," said Harry. "All of these things are written in blood. And some of them look like fresh blood."

"Maybe it's just a warning to watch out for bats, spiders, and owls," Brian said.

"It's a warning, alright. But I don't think it's a friendly one." Harry's morale had sunk significantly since entering the room.

"Maybe we should leave a note or something," Brian suggested.

"Yeah," said Harry, "let's leave a note inviting the creepy guy to dinner. Maybe he can sleep in your bed tonight too."

Brian took out his pen and wrote a note on a piece of paper:

We are here exploring the area. We are staying at the Mayer's cabin by the farm. If you need help please come see us there. We are leaving tomorrow at noon. We can give you a lift.

Brian ripped the note off of his pad and picked up a rusty nail from the ground. "Give me your gun for a second," he said to Harry. Brian used the butt of the gun to hammer the nail into the wall with the note attached. The nail slid in the compromised wood easily. They withdrew from the room.

"Which way to the exit?" Harry asked.

"This way," Brian said, pointing left, with the gun still in his right hand.

Just then, they hear a loud huffing. It sounded like the flipping of the lips of a big animal. The sound was close, and aggressive. The men stopped. They were not sure what the sound was or where it came from, but they knew it was close. It sounded like it was in stereo or surround sound. Before they could get their bearings, a low, deep growl, that would make any human tremble, resonated from close by. This time, there was no doubt: the sound was coming from behind them. Harry unenthusiastically turns and shines his flashlight in the area of the noise. He shines it just in time to see a large, brown Grizzly bear with his mouth wide open and teeth fully exposed roaring. The roar was so loud that even though the bear was fifteen-yards away the wind from his breath could be felt. The sound echoed and vibrated throughout their bodies.

Without even thinking, Brian raised

his right hand, with his left hand still at his side, and fired a shot at the bear.

Boom!

The recoil from the gunfire sent the gun flying out of Brian's hand and through a crack in the floor. The gun was now irretrievable. Time seemed to stop for the men, or at least move in slow motion. In the heat of the moment, Brian had forgotten the cardinal rule of firing a handgun: *steady the weapon with your off-hand*. Being nervous, however, Brian used only his right arm to fire the gun. The bullet whizzed through the air, zooming by Harry, who was positioned to Brian's right and a couple of steps closer to the bear.

Instead of hitting the bear in his head, as he had aimed for, the bullet hit the bear's right shoulder. Harry's body jerked at the sound of the gunfire. His left ear, now, momentarily inoperable. The bear's right shoulder jerked back slightly, and a puff of hair where the bullet had entered expelled into the air. The bear stood up on his hind legs and let out another roar; this one even louder and more aggressive than the last. It stood nearly eleven-feet tall. The shot had done one thing and one thing only: angered the bear even more.

"Oh, shit, run!" Harry screamed. The two men broke into a full sprint. Brian was slightly ahead of Harry. They ran faster than they had ever imaged they could. They both slipped in certain areas where it was icier than others. Their feet pounded into nearly a foot of water in an area where the ice had melted. They made sharp rights and lefts down narrow corridors, breathing heavily and running for their lives to reach the exit. The narrow hallways and slippery conditions made it even hard for the bear to navigate with impunity. Regardless, the bear was closing in on them in a hurry.

The only thing that seemed to be aiding them in their escape were the sharp turns that they had to make, inadvertently, while running at full speed toward the exit. They made a quick left down the corridor where it split into two directions. However, they would have to make a strategic move soon or at least one of them would be a bloody meal for the 1,000-pound creature. Harry flung his flashlight back at the bear, not looking back to see if it hit him or not.

He then heard it bounce off the ground.

By now, the bear was less than five yards away. Their hearts were racing. Certain death for one of them was literally seconds away. It would likely be Harry caught first, as he was a few steps behind Brian. Closer and closer the bear came. The conflict was looking as though it would inexorably lead to their doom.

"Over there!" Brian bellowed, as he pointed to his left. There was a hole in the ground on the side of the hallway. Brian jumped in first. He turned and reached out to Harry. "Come on!" he shouted, as he saw the bear raise his paw to strike his beloved friend. Harry, the former all-state baseball player, slid toward the hole. The bear leapt forward. His body off the ground, right paw over his head, in striking position. Harry's feet entered the ditch and his body quickly followed. His back and head were still exposed when the bear began to swing his paw forward, looking to strike Harry's head with a deadly blow. With incredible force, the bears claw made contact, making a high-pitched squeaking noise, like nails scrapping across a chalkboard.

The ear-splitting clatter was the sound of the bear's claw scrapping across the metal surrounding the hole. It had narrowly missed Harry's head by no more than an inch. Harry's body fell deeper into the hole, right next to Brian. The two looked up and stayed low. There was just enough room for the two of them. The bear gathered himself and his eyes were soon peering into the dark hole. The bear was now angrier than ever. Following an irritated-sounding roar, the bear reached his left paw into the hole and began flailing it back and forth. The men could hear the *swooshes* of air inches above their heads from the menacing claw.

But that menacing sound was soon eclipsed by a much more violent and much more alarming sound. A bizarrely loud, screeching, "AAAAAHHHHH," sound completely filled the area. The sound is tantamount to a human scream in both pitch and decibel level. Three times the skin-crawling scream/whistle can be heard.

In the midst of the intense caterwauling sound, the bear promptly stops what he is doing. As if panicked, the bear's jaws pop together; his teeth begin clacking. He pulls his arm from the hole, and hurriedly runs back from where he had come. At that moment, there was complete silence. The men looked at each other, confused. They said nothing, just listened. After a minute or so Brian slowly stuck his head out of the hole and quickly panned the area, as if he was about to cross a two-lane highway. Harry continued to crouch motionlessly. He was still in complete shock and trying to process what had just happened.

"He's gone," Brian said, just above a whisper.

Brian climbed out of the hole and continued to look around. Harry still hadn't moved.

"Come on," Brian said, as he motioned to Harry.

"What the fuck was that sound, bro?" Harry asked, in a low, but agitated voice. Harry had now begun to exit the hole.

"I don't know, man," Brian responded.

"That was literally the creepiest shit I ever heard," said Harry, in a frantic sounding voice.

"Shh," Brian uttered with a whisper. "What's that noise?"

They looked down the hallway. It was too dark to see very far. In the distance they heard low squeaking noises and what sounded like an approaching gust of wind. It grew louder by the second.

"What is that, man?" Harry said anxiously.

"I don't know," said Brian. "Quiet!"

They waited and waited as the sound grew closer and closer. The squeaking noise and the sound of extremely high wind had soon became evident to Brian. Yet, before he could muster-up the energy to say what he was thinking, his light caught a glimpse of what was rapidly approaching.

"Oh shit, back in the hole!" Brian shouted.

"*BATS!*"

Brian jumped back in the hole as he was shouting those words. Harry stood for a second like a deer in headlights. He had his flashlight in that direction and was squinting to get a better look. It took a second or two for his brain to process what

Brian had just voiced.

"BATS?" Harry screamed.

Before he could get the full word out, he made a quick move toward the hole. But before he did, he was overwhelmed with bats flying in his face and all around him. Fluttering wings and loud chirps and squeaks soon drowned-out any other sounds.

Harry managed to get in the hole.

"Oh, God!" he screamed, as he managed to take two bats along with him in the hole. One was stuck on his leg. The other, on his shirt. With its teeth showing and its mouth open, it lunged toward Harry's face, making a high-pitched squeaking noise. Brian quickly grabbed the one on his leg and threw it up and out of the hole. Harry was screaming and waving his arms around in a panic. Brian quickly grabbed the other bat and threw it out as well.

"Now I got rabies! I got rabies!" Harry shouted, as he frantically brushed himself off in disgust.

"Oh, stop it," Brian said. "Just stay low. They will pass."

Thousands upon thousands of bats worked their way through the hallway. It was a sea of bats. So many, that bats were all that could be seen. Within a few minutes, the hallway was dead silent again and the bats were gone.

"Guess now we know what the bat drawings were for?" said Brian.

"H-a, h-a," Harry uttered sarcastically. "Very funny. Let's get the hell out of here, please, before spiders and owls come next."

Chapter 9

Writing on the Wall

The gun sits on the living room coffee table. Next to it, a bottle of wine, almost empty. Sarah is sitting on the big couch. Laurie is sitting on the love seat. They've finally found a way to relax, amid the day's stressful events. For the last hour they have been drinking wine, Pinot Grigio. Their earlier adventure has been set aside momentarily.

"What's your favorite 90's band," asked Sarah.

"My favorite 90's group is definitely *The Red Hot Chili Peppers*," Laurie reveals. "I saw them many times. One of the best was the *Tibetan Freedom Concert* in D.C. It was a two-day concert, Saturday and Sunday. I went on a Sunday. The Chili Peppers were supposed to play the day before, but the weather was bad and lightning actually struck one of the people in the audience, and that person died. So, obviously they canceled the rest of the acts for that day, which included the Peppers. So, I go Sunday. I'm like, okay, it's *REM*, *Pearl Jam*, *Blues Traveler*, *Beastie Boys*, and *A Tribe Called Quest*. So, Pearl Jam headlined, and they just finished their last song. They were amazing. And everyone started walking out.

We were half-way up the aisle, and then you hear a quick thump from a bass guitar, loud. It was like they were saying, 'hold on a second.' I mean, it was an all-day concert, so people were tired and ready to leave at that point. We all turned around and you see a bunch of guys on stage. I screamed, 'oh my God, it's Flea!' And then you hear the funky guitar riff, and then

Anthony Kiedis sings, 'Hey batter, batter, batter, swing.' And everyone ran back to their seats and the Peppers played an incredible set. The surprise factor was very intense. People were going nuts. What about you?"

"Wow, that's cool. Not to sound all braggadocious and stuff," Sarah said, "but I was at the *Nirvana MTV Unplugged* in 1993. The buzz was just unbelievable. And their performance actually topped the buzz. I've never felt something so electric, as far as shared energy. And what made it even more memorable was that after the show Brian asked me to be his girl."

"So, he asked you to go steady after the concert?"

"Yeah, and we were wasted. But still, it's a day I will never forget, ever."

"That's so sweet! Oh, my goodness! I can't believe we are almost finished with our second bottle of wine." Laurie chuckles.

"Thanks for reminding me," Sarah mentions.

"Let me get another," Sarah said.

Laurie sat back and rested her head. She was very content. The alcohol helped take the edge off. That was until the men came storming through the door. Sarah was walking back into the room with a bottle of wine in hand.

"Oh good, you're back," she says.

"You're never gonna believe what happened to us," Harry said. "First, we got attacked by a bear!"

"What?" shouted Sarah.

"Then we got attacked by bats," Brian said, "and Harry got the worst of it."

"And we heard this creepy sound," Harry says. "It sounded like a scream from a horror movie, but not like a female scream, it was just crazy!"

"And we found a room in the mine where it looked like someone was there recently," said Brian.

"Recently?" Laurie responded. "How could you tell that?"

"Because there was smoke from a fire that had just been put out."

"What?" asked Sarah.

"And there were several spooky hand-written pictures on the wall," Harry said.

"And we think it was written in

blood," said Brian.

"Okay, you guys are seriously killing my buzz!" Sarah said.

"Maybe it's the guy Dizzy dropped off here," Laurie suggested. "I saw that guy again out front. Maybe he is scared to approach us."

"Something is not right here," said Sarah.

"I think that we should just relax here for the night," Harry said. "We have one gun, food and drinks. We can just hunker down and leave tomorrow."

"What do you mean we have 'one gun?'" asked Sarah.

"I dropped the other gun while we were being chased by the bear," Brian revealed. "It's gone."

"You dropped the gun?" Sarah shouted. "Are you kidding me?"

"You try getting chased by a large grizzly, see how you keep it together," Brian said, annoyed.

"okay, okay, I'm holding this gun," Harry says, as he picks up the Glock and puts it behind his back with his right hand; sticking it in his pants, between his back and belt.

"I left my cigarettes upstairs," said Sarah. "I'll be right back. Sarah walked up the stairs. Her footsteps can clearly be heard above from the creaky floor.

Then the group heard a loud-

-*BOOM*!

"What the hell was that?" Laurie shouted.

"Shh," Brian uttered.

All three of them stayed quiet and focused in on their hearing, waiting for any sounds. Their muscles tightened; their breathing slowed. After a minute, they spoke.

"It was probably just a rock or something blowing into the house," said Harry. "It is windy out."

Only moments later they heard another-

-*BOOM!*

This one was even louder.

"What the fuck was that?" Harry yelled.

"Let's go outside and check," Brian said. Harry grabbed the gun with his right hand. He hit the magazine release and the magazine slid down the handle of the gun. Harry looked to make sure it was loaded. It was. He popped the magazine back in place. Brian grabbed a metal fireplace poker off the stand near the chimney. He gripped it tightly and gave it a half-swing, for practice.

"Okay," Brian said," let's go."

"Stay here," Harry said to Laurie.

The men walked out the front door.

"It sounded like it came from over here," Brian said, pointing to the right.

It was pitch black outside. Even with a flashlight it was hard to see more than a few feet in any direction. Harry had flung his flashlight at the bear back at the mine, so they were down to three flashlights. They walked cautiously around to the side of the house. Brian had the poker in his right hand, in striking position. Harry had the gun drawn with his right hand on the weapon. In his left hand he held a flashlight that he held against the gun for point of aim. His arms held stiffly in front of him in case he needed to fire quickly. They walked slowly around to the side of the house, but there was no one there.

"Who the fuck is out here?" Harry

screamed. "I am armed. You don't wanna fuck with me."

"If anyone is out there," said Brian, "we are not gonna hurt you. We have food and water if you need. Just show yourself."

Brian surveyed the area where he thought the sound came from. He saw two big rocks laying close to the house. Harry aimed the flashlight on the side of the house to see if there was any damage.

"Brian, look at this," Harry shouted.

On the side of the house were words, written in blood:

'Are you Listening Yet?'

"Yo, someone is fucking with us now, it's official," said Harry.

"It's the same hand-writing as from the mine," Brian pointed out.

"You're a fucking handwriting specialist to now?"

"No," Brian said. "It's easy to see. Plus, I doubt there's a list of people here writing shit in blood." Harry bobbed his head, conceding to the point. The men then went around to the back of the house and secured the perimeter. They found no one.

"Let's get back inside," said Brian.

The men headed back inside, visibly shaken. They were in a strange place at night. They have no electricity. They have no idea who is out there or how many, but they have just realized that at least one person has just fired the first shot, hypothetically. This is war. However, it's a war that they are very reluctant to entertain. Home field advantage is real.

Back at the cabin, the men bang on the door. Laurie opens it brusquely.

"What happened?" she asks.

"Nothing," Harry says.

"What do you mean, nothing?" Laurie asks.

"No one was there," Harry responds.

"Where is Sarah?" Brian asks.

"She is still upstairs," said Laurie.

"Sarah!" Brian screams. "Sarah!" Brian screams again.

"I'm going to check on her," Brian says.

Harry's face looked pale. He was not himself and Laurie noticed.

"What's wrong?" she asked. "What

happened out there?"

"Nothing, everything is fine."

"You are acting weird," Laurie pronounced. "Tell me what's going on, now!" she declared.

"Someone wrote, 'Are you listening yet?' on the side of the house. Someone is out there messing with us."

"I told you," Laurie said. "We have no idea what we are up against." Brian comes running down the stairs frantically.

"She's not up there," he says. Brian is now noticeably terrified.

"What do you mean she is not up there?" Laurie asks.

"She is not there. I looked everywhere."

Laurie runs upstairs to look for Sarah.

"Sarah!" she screams. "Sarah!" But there is no answer. She searches under the beds and in the closets, but finds nothing. Her flashlight starts flickering. She smacks it against her leg and it shines bright once again. She shines it out the window, where she had originally seen the figure. This time she sees Sarah.

She squints her eyes. She can't really

see much, only Sarah flailing around with her flashlight in hand. Then, she sees the unthinkable. Behind her, the figure has his right forearm around her neck. Sarah is struggling to break free. Sarah sees the light from Laurie's flashlight and starts screaming and trying to shake loose as best she can. It looks like she is calling for help. Laurie tries to open the window, but it won't budge. It's been painted shut. She shines the light out the window again, but they're gone. She races down the stairs desperately to tell the others.

"I just saw her!" she screams. "She was in the yard being restrained by that guy!"

"What?" Brian says. Brian grabs the poker and runs to the front door without a thought. Harry and Laurie follow close behind. Total chaos has now broken out. What was once a possible threat has now become the worst-case scenario. Things had happened so fast that it was impossible to process in real time.

Brian flings the door open and runs to the back of the house.

"Sarah!" he screams.

"Sarah!" he bellows again into the night. "I'm gonna kill you, you mother fucker! Give me back my wife!" His screams echoed into the darkness. While Brian is screaming, Laurie goes into a momentary trance-like state. Her eyes roll to the top of her head. Before the other two could notice, she was back to normal.

"I just saw her," Laurie said. "He took her to the mine."

"What do you mean you just saw her?" Harry asked, puzzled.

"I don't know," Laurie said. "I have been feeling strange ever since passing out in the basement. It's like I'm sharing my eyes with someone else...like, like someone else is using my eyes as well."

"What do you mean, passed out?" said Harry.

"It's a long story," Laurie says.

"I'm going back to the mine," Brian says adamantly. "She has to be there. Let's go!" Brian heads to the back yard, without pause, in the direction of the mine.

"We don't know if she's there or not," Harry cried.

"What other options do we have?"

Brian retorted. "That's the only place we know, and we know he was there."

"I need a weapon," Laurie says.

"We don't have time," Harry says.

"We will protect you. Just grab a stick or something."

Brian falls to one knee a few yards ahead, and about 30 yards from the back of the house. Harry and Laurie run over to him.

"What is it?" Laurie asks. Brian starts crying and becoming more unhinged by the second. He points to the ground. Laurie and Harry aim their flashlights in the direction that Brian pointed. There were two long, evenly marked longitudinal striations or grooves in the dirt, parallel to one another, indicating two feet were dragged across the surface. The drag marks went on for about five to ten yards.

"I found this," Brian said weeping. He held up Sarah's muddy sneaker.

"Oh my God!" shouted Laurie.

"Let's go!" Harry yelled. "We gotta go get her!"

Then, a loud scream echoed into the night. It sounded like it was nearby; but the group knew right away that it wasn't Sarah's scream. It was a creepy, devilish scream. Laurie spun around, looking to be attacked by the owner of the scream.

"That's the sound we heard in the mine," Harry shouted.

"Yeah," Brian agreed, "the same exact scream."

"That's no scream, guys," Laurie offered.

"Huh?" Harry asked.

"That's a whistle," said Laurie.

"A whistle?" Harry asked confused.

"She's right," Brian agreed. "That's the Aztec death whistle. Oh no, please!" Brian broke down again.

"That's the whistle Dizzy warned us of," said Laurie, "remember? He said if it sounds close it's far away and..."

"Yeah, yeah," Harry interjected, "and if it sounds far away it's close. Okay, so let's hurry. It came from this way," Harry said, pointing toward the mine. "And it sounded close."

"Which means he is far away," Laurie said.

"Let's go!" Brian screamed.

What's "Mine" is Yours

They hurried through the small wooded area that led to the steep hill leading to the entrance of the mine. By now, they had little fear for themselves. Their only thought was to retrieve Sarah alive and keep the group together until Dizzy arrived for them at noon. At no time did they think that Sarah could be dead. Really, they just didn't have time to process things. It all happened in the blink of an eye. The only way to salvage this was to get Sarah back. The thought of going home without her never crossed their minds.

No one even thought to mention or postulate how Sarah could have been taken so quickly and quietly from the second floor of the cabin, unheard or unseen. Particularly when Laurie had been in the living room, next to the stairs, while the men were at the side of the house checking on the noises. They had to first deal with the reality that Sarah was gone. Moreover, they believed that they only had a short window to retrieve her before something really bad happened. The thought of leaving this place without her was not an option for any of them. If that meant Brian fighting that bear with his bare hands then so be it.

They reached the mine entrance in minutes. All three walked the balance beam and squeezed through the tiny make-shift entrance with no fear of falling. Every second that passed the morale of the three dissipated a bit.

"How do we know for sure that he took her here?" Harry asked.

"We don't," Brian responded. "But this is the only place we know. Plus, we know they were headed in this direction."

"Oh my God!" Laurie shouts, as she stopped and pointed her flashlight to the ground. There, she had found Sarah's other sneaker.

"Holy shit!" Harry exclaimed. As soon as Brian saw the sneaker he began running, furiously, toward the room he had seen the hand-drawings and smoke. The other two tried to keep up with him, but Laurie was having trouble with the slippery conditions. Furthermore, it was now night-time, so visibility was even worse than before. And this was Laurie's first time in the mine, so she had no idea what the conditions were like. *BAM!*

Laurie slips and falls to the ground.

"Ow, my knee!" she screams. Harry stops to assist her. He grabs her arm.

"Are you okay?" Harry helps her up, as she begins to assess the damage.

"Yeah, I think I'm alright," Laurie says. Harry picks up her flashlight and hands it back to her. Laurie wipes herself off a bit. Some mud had gotten on her pants and elbow. By now, Brian was long gone. The two, now regrouped from Laurie's fall, had now realized that Brian had gone way ahead. They ran as fast as they could, convinced that staying together was best for all of them, in case there was more than one attacker.

As they turn the corner, Harry noticed the room with the two clay statues at the entrance. He noticed a bright light emanating from inside the room. Of course, Brian did have a flashlight, but this was brighter than one flashlight would produce. As they sprinted into the room, they saw Brian standing there, staring at the embers of the low fire. This time it burned higher than before. They were sure that someone had been there after their last visit.

"He was here," Brian said, in a calm and defeated-sounding voice.

"With Sarah?" Harry asked. Brian nodded his head up and down, his back still to Laurie and Harry. "How do you know?" Harry asked.

Brian holds up a shirt with his right hand. It was Sarah's shirt. Harry put his head in his left hand.

"What's that over there?" Laurie asked. She pointed to a bag sitting off to the left. The bag was white and very dirty. It also appeared to be half filled with something.

"Bones," Brian said, nonchalantly.

Laurie walked over and knelt down. She opened the bag.

"What the hell," she said. "Oh my God!"

"What is it?" Harry asked.

"It's filled with human bones," Laurie said.

At that moment, the group heard that chilling whistle that resembled the scream of a demon. This time, it sounded far away.

Brian turned his head, facing Laurie and Harry. His eyes red and squinting. His lips narrowed to the point where it looked like he was biting them. His eyebrows were tilted toward the center of his face. He all but snarled.

"I'm gonna get that fucking prick!" Brian shouted. He brushed up against Harry during his sprint out of the room. He nearly pushed Harry over. By the time the other two had processed what just happened, Brian was gone.

"Brian, wait!" Harry shouted. Harry and Laurie ran out of the room and followed the winding corridor. Laurie trailed just behind Harry. Two more eerie whistles rang-out during their pursuit. Both sounded far away. Within a few seconds they had located Brian standing about twenty-yards away, down the dark corridor, where it split. One could either go left or right. Brian stood peering further down the left hallway with his flashlight, which is where the three had entered from.

"Brian, wait!" Harry screamed.

"Over here," he responded. He turned to face his friends. "I saw someone run down this way."

Just then, Laurie and Harry see a figure in the dark appear behind Brian. The figure is tall and gaunt. Standing about six-feet-four-inches. The figure wore a hoodie with the hood over his head, making it difficult to get a good look at his face.

"Brian, behind you!" Laurie cried.

Brian turned and looked at the face of the figure. The moment Brian turned to face the figure; a large knife was thrust into his stomach. Brian lets out a groan. All of the 15-inch blade is driven deep into his stomach. He drops the flashlight in a puddle of water. It flickers twice, then goes dead. Brian slumps forward and begins to gasp and choke. The figure stands, holding the knife in Brian with his right hand, while staring at the other two. Harry is in complete shock, still trying to understand what he was witnessing. These two had grown up together. They were the best of friends. They were supposed to grow old together. Their whole relationship flashed through Harry's mind in only a second or two.

"Brian!" Laurie yelled, with an aching scream.

"NO!" Harry roared with a prolonged scream.

The figure let out a screeching, aggressive shriek at the two, and then a squelching sound can be heard as he pulled the knife from Brian's near-lifeless body. The serrated back portion of the blade tore skin, bone, and portions of Brian's organs out of his body. Blood squirted out of his stomach and ran from his mouth. Brian fell to the ground. He coughed repeatedly, spraying blood from his mouth. There was no thought put into his coughs. It was just his body reacting to the blood in his throat that was choking him to death.

Harry reached back for his gun. He pulled it out and ran toward the figure. He began firing it as he started running. With his adrenalin racing toward its limit, the first two shots he fired went high. The Glock can fire every bullet in the clip rapidly. Harry continued firing. Shots rang-out.

BANG, BANG, BANG...

One hit the figure in the right

shoulder. Immediately after, another hit him in his right shoulder. The figure let out a scream. The barrel of Harry's gun snapped back, indicating that the gun was empty. In his haste, Harry forgot to bring an extra clip or bullets. Harry paid no mind. He kept running toward the figure. Laurie was now the one in shock. She stood motionless.

"Harry!" she screamed.

Harry was running fast enough that the light on his flashlight was dancing around the corridor. The figure let out another loud, aggressive screeching sound. It then turned its head to its left [*ZING,* a blur]. Harry reached Brian. He looked right, then left. His flashlight followed his eyes as he quickly looked both ways. The figure was gone!

Chapter 10

Things will never be the same

For everyone, there is a moment in time that marks the most pivotal moments in a person's life. It's a line that's drawn. An epoch in their history. That line signifies 'before this and after this.' That moment when things are forever changed. For some it represents the age of innocence. In modern time it's the birth of Jesus Christ of Nazareth (BC & AD). For Harry and Laurie, their line had just been drawn.

They now knew for sure that something had been hunting them. Harry dropped to his knees.

"Brian!" he screamed, in a desperate voice.

Laurie had caught up to Harry and

was now standing behind him. With Brian lying in the fetal position, he tried to cover the large hole in his stomach. Harry gently put his hand on Brian's shoulder.

"Hang in there buddy. It's gonna be okay." Harry paused for a second. A tear ran down his cheek. "Can you move?" he asked. Brian shook his head side to side. Then, Brian reached for Harry with his left hand. Harry stood and grabbed his arm and tried to help him up. However, the agony was too much, even for a slight movement. Brian's legs gave out after only a slight jolt. He was too weak to stand. Harry gently placed him back down. Brian rolled onto his back.

"Find Sarah, please," Brian pleaded, as he struggled to push the words from his mouth. By now, the tears running down Harry's cheeks had greatly multiplied. He knew that this was the end of the road for his buddy, and the last time he would see him again on this earth, even though the weight of that had not yet sunken in.

"Don't you worry, buddy," Harry said, with tears in his eyes.

"We had a good run, didn't we,"

Brian barely managed to say. Blood splattered out of his mouth with every syllable.

"We had the best run, Bri. I promise you, I'm gonna find Sarah. Don't you worry," Harry stated confidently, but inside half-heartedly.

Just as Harry finished his last sentence, Brian started coughing violently. Within seconds, his eyes rolled to the back of his head and the coughing stopped.

Brian was gone!

"NO!" Harry screamed. His scream echoed down every corridor. Laurie put her hand on Harry's shoulder. Harry stood up and hugged Laurie. His tears soaked her shoulder.

"We should get going," Laurie said, after a few moments.

Harry exhaled raggedly. "Yeah, yeah," he whimpered softly.

As they exited the mine, Laurie remained keenly aware of her surroundings. She kept her head on a swivel. She knew that this thing was still out there and hunting them. Harry had checked-out for the moment. He was still in shock, and had lost all hope momentarily. He was running on pure instinct and adrenaline. He had just lost his two closest friends. They were more than just friends, actually. They were like family. Harry really had no one else his whole life. The moment was just too big for him. Yet, Laurie knew that he needed to regain his composure or they would both be dead soon.

They made their way through the small wooded area that leads to the path that leads to the cabin.

"Come on, come," Laurie shouted. "This way!" She pulled Harry's arm and he waddled forward. Once the cabin was in sight, they raced to get inside. Harry came alive about twenty-yards from the front door. His eyes blinked rapidly and he looked over each shoulder to see what was around him. He appeared to have awoken suddenly. He compartmentalized Brian's death and refocused the gravity of the situation. 'He would have time to lament later,' he thought to himself.

Cabin Fever

They raced into the cabin and closed the door. Harry locked it. Laurie lit up four candles and put the matchbox in her front-right pocket.

"Stay away from the window," Harry said. "We are gonna get through this!"

Harry reached into the blue duffle bag and grabbed the fully-loaded gun-clip that had ten-rounds in it (the max that one clip can hold) and loaded the gun. He then grabbed the empty clip and began loading it. He had two clips, total. He stuck the newly loaded clip in the back-left pocket of his jeans and laid the loaded gun on the table. He sat down, took a deep breath, and then let out a *ragged exhalation*. The room was extremely dark. The candles served as a beacon of light only for a short distance.

"We should be safe in here until morning," Harry said. "As long as we stay put."

Laurie walked around the first floor making sure that the house was secure. Just before she returned to the living room, a loud crash penetrated the deafening silence. The window in the living room shattered, followed by a resounding thud and three more faint thuds. Laurie aimed her flash light in the direction where she heard the last thud.

Laurie let out a loud, harrowing scream, as she recognized that it was Sarah's head that had just been violently thrown through the living room window.

Harry Inhales sharply.

"What is it?" he shouts.

Laurie begins walking backwards, away from Sarah's severed head. She is flummoxed and speechless. She has her hand over her mouth and is gasping rapidly. Harry runs over and shines his flashlight on Sarah's detached head.

"Oh, God!" he cries.

Laurie runs behind Harry, who is pointing the gun shakily at the front door with his right hand and reaching around with his left to secure Laurie.

Laurie fretfully scans the room. Her eyes graze by the stairs, and then quickly back, focusing on the top of the staircase leading to the second floor. There, stands the hooded figure, staring at her ominously.

"Up there!" she screams. "The stairs!"

Harry quickly turns to his left and begins firing.

BANG, BANG, BANG...

The fleet-footed figure darts down the stairs and runs toward the kitchen area. Harry continues firing until the figure is out of sight. The blurring speed in which the figure exhibits confuses and further frightens the couple. All three candles went out simultaneously as the figured moved toward the kitchen area. Making matters worse, Harry had fired five of the ten rounds in the clip, all unsuccessfully.

Dead silence and darkness further aid to the treacherousness of the situation. Harry walks forward. Laurie still directly behind him. Harry has the gun aiming forward and nervously waving the flashlight around, trying to hold it steady.

Holding the gun in his right hand and the flashlight in the other, Harry tip toes forward, trying to get the jump on the figure. Laurie is exhaling rapidly; Harry is breathing slowly, trying to remain calm for the sake of shooting accurately.

Harry remembers his father teaching him how to shoot. Of the many words of advice, he recalls his father telling him, *"Slow your heart rate. Calm yourself. It's the man who stays calm who has the advantage in a gunfight."* Even knowing this advice was true, Harry was still having a hell of a time trying to remain calm. With all the terrible things that have happened in just a short time, Harry was a mess inside. Moreover, they didn't even know what they were up against, and they were in a foreign place with no help in sight. They both also had a strange feeling from what they had witnessed thus far, that something was bizarre about this showdown. Was this the monster that lives under our beds or the one that has been in the nightmares of every human being since the dawn of time? All the horrible things that he has done, and they still haven't even gotten a good look at him yet.

They slowly pass the staircase when they hear another window smash. This time, it sounds like it had come from the dining room. They rounded the corner and passed the kitchen. They headed toward the family room, passing the bathroom along the way. They were running out of real estate. Their hearts raced faster, as they knew a confrontation was seconds away.

In the dining room, they noticed that the window was broken. Laurie ran up to the window and saw a chair had been thrown through it. Harry continued securing the room.

"He went out this way," Laurie said, pointing toward the broken window.

Harry walked over and looked.

"But how could he have gotten out?" Harry asked, sounding confused. "Only the middle portion of the window is broken."

They both hear running footsteps approaching quickly. Harry turns around and points the gun back toward the kitchen. The figure runs at Harry and lunges forward. Harry shoots once, *BANG,* hitting the figure in the side of his neck. Blood splatters in all directions. The figure's lunge was unobstructed by the strike, however. He grabbed Harry's arm with his left hand and attempted to shake the gun loose. Harry dropped the flashlight, causing a thud on the ground before it went dark. Harry needed both hands to try and maintain control of the pistol. Laurie lets out a prolonged scream. She shines her flashlight on the squabble. As she does, the figure raises his right hand and *smacks* Harry in the face. Harry is hit so hard that both of his feet come off the ground. He slams into the wall and hits the ground, motionless. The gun flew from his hand and hit off the wall. It slid and landed at Laurie's feet. Their eyes are drawn to the gun simultaneously, before their bodies have time to react.

Laurie quickly reaches for the gun, but the figure grabs her by her shirt and lifts her off the ground. Laurie screams and tries to dislodge his hand, to no avail. She swings the flashlight and hits him in the head. She swings again, but this time the figure knocks her arm away. She drops her flashlight. He lifts her up to where she is now face to face with him.

He is facing down, and the front of his hood is still covering his face. He slowly brings his head up. Even though it is now pitch black, she looks forward and sees a gruesome sight.

His eyes are glowing and are spaced far apart. His eyeballs are extremely large, disproportionally larger compared to the size of his entire eye, in fact. His nose is small, but his mouth stretches across the entire front of his face. He opens his mouth and a ghastly sight emerges. His mouth, which is filled with razor-sharp canine teeth, are dripping with bile. He looks into her eyes. She is frozen with fear.

"Let me go!" she cries. "What do you want from us?" she bellowed. The monster opens his mouth and let out a screeching, aggressive shriek. The fetid, acrid smell of his breathe nearly knocks Laurie out, on its own.

No Escape

The shock of the moment made Laurie's mind wander. Her eyes rolled back and she became dizzy and disoriented. The ornery monster sniffed her, as if he was enjoying the satisfying, up close aroma of fear. He was savoring the moment. It had been a while since he had bathed in human blood.

Just as all seemed lost for Laurie, Harry appeared behind the monster, with a devilish look in his eyes. He had reached his breaking point. Fear had left his body. Only rage remained. Harry raised his right hand stiffly. In it, a granite guardian lion statue. He swung it with all his might.

BOOM!

It struck the back of the monster's head and crumbled. The Monster dopped Laurie and turned ominously. The blow had only managed to anger the beast.

"Run!" Harry screamed.

"What about—"

"Run!" he screamed again.

Laurie ran around the monster and past Harry. The monster's focus was solely on Harry now. Laurie hears the monster's scream just before she reaches the front door.

"Come on, you ugly mother fucker," Harry shouts.

Laurie bolts out the door and runs desperately toward the town. She stops about a twenty-five yards from the house.

She turns to try and get a glimpse of Harry. She did not want to leave him, but she had no choice. She wasn't going to be much of a presence in a physical confrontation. Her only method of survival was to flee.

Just as Laurie looks back, she witnesses Harry's lifeless body flying through the broken window. His limbs shook awkwardly through the air. After she heard the THUD from his body hitting the ground, she turned and ran with all her might.

Sole Survivor

Fear stricken; she ran down Main Road moving east. Crying profusely, she knew to survive that she would need to get it together and come up with a plan. As she ran, she thought of a strategy. She knew two things for certain: one, the monster was much stronger than her; and two, he knew the territory better than she did. She remembered the story that Dizzy told them. Her reason for recalling that was to try and find a weakness or a vulnerability in the creature.

She ran past the intersecting Route 9, then slowed her pace a bit. She looked for a place to hide. Visibility was dreadful. She could only see a few feet in front of her. She ran to the school on the left. She pulled on the large door handles, but the doors were locked. Frantically, she looked back to see if her attacker was near. With no site of him, she continued to the convenience store. Although that door was locked as well, the front display window was broken. She entered through it.

The place was in shambles. There were large holes in the roof, revealing the night's sky. The full moon could be seen through the hole in the roof, actually aiding in visibility. Scattered debris an inch thick covered the floors. *CRUNCH, CRUNCH*, can be heard with every step. The smell of rot and mold filled the air. She walked past a sign on the floor reading "Caramelo (Taffy)."

Three of the four aisles of shelves had fallen on one another. Only one aisles of shelves stood, bare. She looked around for a weapon of sorts. She walked behind the counter and found a baseball bat. She grabbed it then ran to the back of the store and found a good hiding spot. The eerie silence would debilitate most people. But not Laurie. She was busy thinking of a plan. She knew she had plenty of time to rehash and mourn the night's events. But she had to survive first.

'*DOGS!*' she thought.

Dizzy had mentioned something about the monster being afraid of dogs. Laurie remembered that she had treated a pesky dog in her office that would not stop barking. No matter what she tried, the unruly dog barked fiercely and consistently. He did not play nice with other dogs, and hearing and smelling other dogs in the building sent him into a non-stop barking frenzy. Laurie had recorded the dog's incessant barking on her phone to show its owner and for documentation purposes.

A skin-crawling scream/whistle breaks the silence. The sound was distant. Laurie knew the creature was close. Seconds later, she heard the first *CRUNCH* on the floor. The monster had arrived. Had he picked up her scent? Or was he just checking every building in the area?

Regardless, he was there, and it would be only moments before he found her.

Laurie gently placed the bat on the ground and pulled out her cell phone. She lowered the brightness on her phone and searched for the barking dog video. The creature was approaching. A loud *CRUNCH* could be heard as he stepped on the *Caramelo* sign. Then, the footsteps stopped. The creature scanned the room. With little time to spare, Laurie found the video. She turned her media audio to full blast and hit play.

"*Woof-woof, ruff-ruff-ruff.*"

The monster shook with fear. Her timing seemed propitious. He looked around quickly to see which direction the dog was coming from. Seconds later, Laurie could hear the sound of footsteps rapidly receding. She played the video for another few seconds, then hit stop. She listened for a moment, even glanced out from her hiding spot twice. When she realized the monster was gone, she got to her feet and made her way out of the store. With no one in site, she rushed back to the house. She knew she needed to get that gun!

Chapter 11

Staying Alive

Laurie ran frantically back down Main Road toward the cabin. She looked back and to the sides frequently, trying to thwart an ambush from the monster. Coming upon the cabin door, Laurie was weary. She knew that the monster had shown up there a few times already. It was very likely that he would be there again. Nonetheless, Laurie believed that her only hope was to find the gun that had fell on the floor in the family room.

Laurie walked slowly through the pitch-black living room. Dead silence, once again. She moved warily past the staircase and through the foyer. It grew darker still as she entered the dining room. She had finally reached the family room. Her first order of business was to find the flashlight she had dropped. Just then, a loud metallic thud sounded next to her. She jumped. Her heart raced. She inhaled sharply. She then realized that she had bumped into a metal object that was on the table and knocked it on the floor. She took a deep breath and let out a sigh of relief.

She carefully dropped to her knees and started searching the floor with her hands in the area where she believed she had dropped her flashlight. Her hand grazed a metal object, pushing it away slightly. She patted around in search of it. She located it with her hands and grabbed a hold. It was not the flashlight. It was the gun!

She had found one of the two survival tools she was searching for. She put it in her waste. Within seconds, she located a flashlight. She clicked the button to turn it on, but no light shined. She slapped it lightly against her open palm. Still, no light. She then realized that the flashlight she was holding was the one that Harry had dropped. She doubled back and finally located her flashlight near the south-west portion of the wall. She clicked the switch up and the light went on. She lets out another breathe, declaratively.

Laurie stood to her feet with the active flashlight and turned toward the dining room. There, in full view of the light, stood the nauseating creature standing in the foyer area. Laurie lets out a scream and starts panting heavily. The creature rushes. The pitter-patter of his feet meant he was moving fast. He was hardly touching the ground. Laurie aims the gun at him and fires.

BANG!

The kick from the shot makes the bullet go high, missing the creature. Laurie turns hastily and dives head-first out of the broken window. She lands kind of awkward, which disoriented her momentarily. She shook it off and realized that her head had luckily landed on top of Harry's stomach, cushioning her head from smacking the ground. However, this was no consolation to her at this moment. She was horrified, and tears streamed from her eyes. She looked up. In the window stood the monster with a menacing glare. He turned and walked away from the window. Laurie knew she only had a few moments before he walked out the front door. She searched the ground, anxiously, for the gun she had dropped. Every second she searched brought the creature one step closer to her. Finally, she located it. She tried to get up quickly, but her leg had been slightly hurt during the fall. It was not debilitating, but enough to impede her from running at maximum speed. Regardless, with a slight limp, she moved away from Main Road, headed toward Fisher Ave. In her haste, she forgot to grab the flashlight. It was likely damaged anyway from the impact of the jump.

Laurie ran with all her might. Her leg was sore and hurting. She had taken quite a fall. But her fast-pumping adrenaline allowed her to run faster than she should have been able to. Large clouds of cold air coursed from her mouth in rapid succession, rising and expanding into the sky. She was desperate. She looked for any shelter, any hiding place from her dreaded foe. She prayed that the building ahead would offer such comforts. Her prayers were answered, as she pulled the door open. As luck would have it, her prayers had led her to the church.

She quickly heads up the long aisle leading to the altar. She passes pew after pew, until she is able to spot the altar in the dark. Her eyes adjust, but it is still hard to see. When she arrives at the altar, she notices some small chunks of fresh meat and blood all over it. As luck would have it, three candles still remain on the alter. She found one that still looks usable. Laurie pulls the match box from her front-right pocket and attempts to light the wick. She holds the flame up against the wick until it burns down to her fingers.

"Ouch!" she utters, just above a whisper.

She throws the match on the floor and tries again with an unused one.

"Come on, come on," she begs. She holds the match like she did the one before. Again, it burns down to her fingers. This time, she throws it out before she feels the burn. With each try she grows more and more desperate. She knows time is not on her side. She again pulls out a match and scrapes it along the striker. She watches as the light burns on the wick, but without catching. Lower and lower the flame burns on the matchstick.

Until...poof!

She walks and looks around with her lit candle. The church is narrower than most churches people are used to. There are three floors in the church. Each can be accessed by one of two sets of stairs, one on each wall, on opposite sides of the altar. While facing the altar, Laurie walks to the left and takes the stairs up, looking for a good hiding spot. Of course, the third floor would be ideal for such an occasion.

The church stands at the intersection of Fisher Ave and Church St. No other buildings happen to be on Church St. The only other establishments located on or just off of Church are one-story community housing cabins. Most are off-road a bit.

An eerie creaking sound echoes as she tip-toes up the stairs. She tries to stay focused, but her mind wanders. Images of Harry pop in her head, unintentionally. Like the first time they met. Their relationship flashes before her eyes. She shakes her head and tries to remain focused. She knows that to get out of this situation she will need to remain sharp, and have her wits about her.

As she reaches the third floor, she immediately notices several chairs stacked up, blocking the entrance to the balcony, which stands above the altar. It also leads to the staircase on the other side. She looks at the bottom of the chairs and slowly looks upward. She notices something odd in her view. It is just above the horizon-line of the stacked chairs. It looks like two feet and legs. She focuses her gaze and sees what looks like a man tied up, hanging from the ceiling. It takes her a few seconds to process.

It is Brian!

An uncontrollable scream leapt from her throat and lips. Brian is hanging high over the altar. His legs and arms are spread. All four of his limbs are tied individually to each side of the church, using four separate ropes. His stomach had been ripped open, and his insides dripped down to the altar. What made it worse, if possible, was the fact that by now she realized that the blood and chunks of meet she saw on the altar was dripping down from above.

Before she could fully process the nightmarish scene, the dreaded whistle/scream sounded. And worse; it sounded like it was far away. She rushes down the stairs to the second floor, being that there was no place to hide on the third floor. She hurriedly nestles herself behind an empty bookshelf and in front of more stacked chairs and debris. Within seconds she hears the church door creak open gingerly. She hears footsteps approaching slowly.

The monster walks up the main aisle, scanning the room along the way. He slowly approaches the left staircase. She could hear each footstep echo as he neared. Before he could take his first step up the staircase, he hears rodents chittering in the direction of the opposite staircase. His head snaps in that direction. His body follows. He doubles his pace toward the opposite stairs. The creature will stop at nothing to get his hands on her!

Chapter 12

Let Us Pray

The monster hurries up the stairs. He enters the small second floor hallway. His movements, aggressive. He turns with purpose, ready to strike. He slows his movements when he realized she is not on that floor. He proceeds to the third floor with even more fervor. He anticipates, through his machinations, that his final victim will be there.

Easy prey!

Laurie tries to remain silent. She leans back to see if she can get a glimpse of her attacker's position through a peak-hole in the debris. She sees nothing. By now the monster had realized that she wasn't on the third floor. Did he miss something on the second floor, he wondered? He quickly heads back to the second floor. He stops and looks a bit more thoroughly this time. Laurie readies the pistol, holding it to her chest. She takes another peek. This time she spots the monster. However, at the same time she sticks her head out to look, the monster looks inadvertently in her direction. The two locked eyes. Both remained motionless, processing the site. Simultaneously, both Laurie and the monster make a mad dash down the stairs.

They both reach the first floor at almost the same time. Laurie heads frantically toward the exit. The monster mimics her movements. They both sprint down the outside ails next to the pews, on opposite sides. Laurie looks at him to see if he is keeping pace.

He is!

As they each reach the final pew, they both turn and are now facing each other. The front door stands in the middle, equal distance from them both. They both stop. They stare at each other like two gunfighters getting ready to face off, like in an old western draw. Whoever makes the first move is likely to set the other in motion as well. A few drops of sticky liquid-drool fall to the floor from the lips of the creature. Laurie is fixated on the hips of the creature. Any slight movement in any direction will tell her in which direction to run in order to avoid him. Laurie takes a deep breath.

Zoom!

She takes off furiously for the front door. The monster follows. It's as though he knows he can beat her. He is toying with her. They both run toward each other like two rams on a collision course to lock horns. Laurie continues forward, fearlessly, as if she is actually going to engage the beast. Her face stiffens. She grimaces with aggression. Without warning she raises the gun with her right hand and begins firing.

BANG, BANG, BANG!

She fires three rounds in rapid succession. The first shot hits the creature in the shoulder. The right side of his body swings back slightly. Yet, he continues unimpeded. The second-round hits the same area, but a little closer to his chest.

The monster keeps coming. The third round, however, hits center mass. The monster lets out a painfully-high-pitched screech, and falls to one knee. His head face down, as if he is trying to regroup. The top of the gun slides back, indicating that the gun is now empty. She sprints through the church doors and out onto the street.

Intensive Care

Laurie sprints down Church Street going east. Her leg is no longer bothering her; although, it certainly will be tomorrow if she is able to survive. Instead of veering left and attempting to settle in one of the several cabins along the way; Laurie continues past the intersecting Route 9. She believes that the further away from the beast she gets the better. Moreover, she believes that picking a hiding spot with more room inside gives her a better chance of not being found. She would have more places to hide and the monster would have more ground to cover to find her. Laurie veers right and heads toward the school. She checks the front door, but it has a chain lock on it. She walks around looking for another door to enter. At the back of the school is another door. She pulls on it twice, but it too is locked. She had tried the convenience store already, but that didn't go so well. So, she keeps moving east.

She comes upon hospital way. She notices the hospital straight ahead. She sprints to the front door and gives it a couple of tugs, to no avail. Her hope begins to fade. She had run far. She was running out of places to hide. She wasn't sure how the creature had tracked her down at every turn. She chalked it up to it being his home turf. He is, of course, familiar with the area. So much so that he had mastered the terrain. Still, Laurie has a strategic mind. Besides, she still has her wits about her, and she was becoming more focused as the confrontation continued.

She looked for another door. A side door, a back door—any door. Yet, she finds only locked doors. Suddenly, her visual focus changes, much like before. Just like that, she is able to see clearer. It is as though there is a clarity to her sight that is unexplainable, inexplicable. She scans the area almost like a computer would. Her eyes seem to slow time slightly, even. It is as though she can see through her eyes with precision, yet, she is not in control. She tells her head where to move, but it moves where it wants to. She feels like her brain is being hacked by some perspicacious entity.

Her head raises and something leads her ocular focus to a second-floor window that is broken. Laurie begins walking toward the drainage pipe that runs up the corner of the building. She begins climbing the delicate pipe, careful not to rip it from the building. 'How am I doing this?' she thought. She is, at this moment, a spectator in her own body. She reaches the second floor. The window is almost a full arms-reach away. She steadies her left foot on the metal piece that holds the drainage pipe to the wall.

She leaps!

The metal piece tears from the concrete, sending the pipe flying. Her right hand grabs onto the ledge directly in front of the window. But her hand begins slipping immediately. She reaches out her left hand and grabs the ledge. Thankfully, the slant of the concrete ledge tilts slightly forward. She is able to secure herself. She pulls up and uses her feet to scale up the wall. She uses her feet to provide leverage in order to spring herself through the window head first.

Thud!

She hits the floor hard. Immediately, she regains total control of her bodily functions and mental capacity. She groans shortly after impact. The grown intensifies as she tries to rise to her feet. She stands and looks around. She landed at the end of the second-floor hallway, which heads in only one direction. It is a long hallway with classrooms on either side. She begins walking, hoping to find an open door. She tries one door after another, but no luck. She soon realizes that she will need to go down to the first floor. There is nowhere to hide on the second floor, just an empty hallway.

She carefully navigates her way down the first-floor staircase. As she enters through the double doors, she notices the boy's bathroom. She makes a left and sees, that immediately to her right is, the gymnasium. To her left is the front door entrance to the school and the principal's office next to that. Straight down that hallway are more classrooms. She figures they are probably locked as well. Her best bet, she thought, is to find a hiding spot in the gym.

She hurries into the gym. The floor is a basketball court, with small windows high up on the left side, above the folded-up bleachers. Straight to the back of the gym is a raised performance stage with a curtain. This will be her best place to hide, she believes. Laurie hops up onto the elevated stage and separates the curtain in the middle. She walks through. The curtain closes behind her, concealing her from view. The stage is cluttered with music equipment and chairs. At the back of the stage is another curtain.

The whistling-scream sounds from far away. The beast is near!

Laurie dashes behind the second curtain and stands steadily between a brick wall and the curtain, in a space about two-feet wide. She hears a creaking sound. She theorizes in her mind what it is, but she's not sure. Moments later, she hears a large thud on the gym floor. The beast had climbed through the creaky window, hung down by his hands and dropped down to the gymnasium floor. She could hear every footstep. At first the steps lead away from the stage. The monster stops for a moment; however, he then heads toward the stage.

Laurie's breathing intensifies as she hears the *thud* from the creature jumping onto the stage. She knows he is close by. The creature begins throwing objects. First, the music stand, which he flings to his right. Then the bass drum, which he flings to his left. He pushes more objects out of his way. He is hoping to scare her into an attempted escape. Laurie's eyes and muscles clench, as she hears the noises close by. She somehow remains completely still, regardless. The curtain she is hiding behind is two-inches off of the ground. She does not realize that her feet are in view under the curtain.

Suddenly, the noises stop. Dead silence. 'Where did he go?' she thought. Moments seem like hours. Laurie thinks that the monster may have left the stage area. She needs to get a look to see where he is before she attempts to change her position. Slowly she pulls the curtain to the side to get a better look. It is very dark and hard to see. A dark shadow to her right seems to be blocking her view. As she looks closer, her worst fear is imagined.

The monster is inches from her face, staring at her furiously.

Laurie moves first. She darts quickly to her left. The monster swings, but misses her. He gives chase, following close behind. She flings chairs and equipment as she maneuvers toward the edge of the stage. Laurie uses the loose stage debris to try and block her attacker. However, the monster dives out and grabs her leg. She kicks and kicks, until the monster lets her loose, momentarily. In the tussle, the arm of his jacket came loose. He stood and angrily tore off the jacket, exposing his naked upper body. Laurie turns and looks. She is frozen for a moment, as she witnesses the nauseating site.

The creature suffers from the worst case of jaundice. His body no longer needs food or water to live. The creature produces no bodily waste. Instead, the carcass slowly rots from within, causing him to show signs of this in the form of skin discoloration, which is yellow and blue. A much slower replicative senescence, however, than occurs in normal humans.

The creature is littered with protuberant veins, visible blood clots in the skin, and small tumors in many areas of his body. His face is somewhat reptilian shaped, although still containing more human characteristics than any others. He does not have hair on his head, and it is somewhat disfigured as well. Inch-thick claws protruded from his fingers. His extra-wide mouth is filled with large canine teeth that can be seen better now than before. And perhaps his most noticeable feature is his large, glowing eyes that emit blue lighting.

Laurie jumps off the stage. She doesn't miss a step as she hits the ground in full sprint. The monster follows close behind. Laurie runs toward the gym exit, while the monster quickly closes the gap. Just as she reaches the exit and begins making a right, the monster grabs her shoulder and spins her around. He throws her on her back and sits on her stomach, straddling her. He begins violently choking her.

Laurie begins to have flashbacks of her uncle assaulting her. The creatures face turns into her uncle's face. She is hallucinating. She remembers the menacing look in her uncle's eyes as he strangled her violently. She thought she was going to die. Her eyes start to well-up with tears. Laurie is quickly losing oxygen. She is only moments away from losing consciousness. Suddenly, her eyes open wide. She grimaces. Her body fills with rage as she remembers her anger toward her uncle. From her inside voice she screams, without making a sound; a foreign language that she has never spoken-

-"*Cualantehua!*" (*"Get off!"*).

The creature is abruptly thrown completely off of Laurie. He slides across the ground and down the stairs, landing at the entrance of the school. Laurie springs up first and resumes a full sprint. She runs to the left, to the staircase she had entered from. Instead of running up the stairs, however, she runs down them. She knows already that there is nowhere to hide on the second floor.

One floor below, she bolts through the door, where she now stands, in the cafeteria. She immediately notices a grotesque, rancid, foul smell; one like she had never smelt before. She continues running forward until she sees what looks like two people sitting at one of the six long tables on the right.

"Hello?" she says. "I need help!" But the figures do not answer. "Hello!" again she asks. Still no response. She walks closer and sees two dead, decaying bodies. One looks like a man, and one like a woman. Both had their guts ripped out and what looked like a bone had been ripped out of each of their legs. She inhales sharply. A brief scream jumped from her lips. She notices that the woman is fully dressed.

She remembers Dizzy's voice describing the couple who had disappeared...

"His wife had on blue jeans, long black boots, and one of those jackets with the fur on the hood. I don't think she knew what she was in for, dressing like that."

The woman had on those exact clothes. Then she remembers Dizzy's voice again...

"The man had on a navy-blue zippered hoodie with chocolate brown cargo pants. You know, the ones with all them pockets on the sides."

She looks over at the man's body. He is wearing only underwear, socks, and a t-shirt. It is at that moment she realizes that the creature was wearing the dead man's pants and hoodie.

Her breathing intensifies and she runs now even faster than before. She enters a very small hallway that leads to a short staircase. She observes a door half way up the stairs, in between the basement and first-floor.

Laurie runs through the double doors so fast that she loses her footing. She falls down the flight of stairs just beyond the door. She rolls and rolls, probably five times. Luckily, this does not slow her down. She is in desperation mode. She feels no pain. Her mind had one singular focus: *escape*.

She runs right toward Main Road. She knows her best chance is to head back to the cabin and retrieve the loaded gun clip. Even though, from what she had witnessed; she didn't believe that the bullets could stop the creature. Regardless, she knew no other weapon she had could. And at least, the bullets could slow him down and provide her with the precious moments she needed to put distance between herself and the creature. Not once did she wonder where she had gotten the strength from to throw the monster off of her. She wasn't even sure what had happened, actually.

Laurie was frustrated. Many other questions ran through her mind. In the absence of any pertinent information on the creature, her only option was to keep running. Yet, she already had several close calls. She knew it was a matter of time before he got a hold of her.

Nevertheless, two important questions remain.

The first question is, how was he tracking her down so quickly? Yes, the town is small. Still, it is a town. And this town has an occupancy of two. There were plenty of places to hide without being found, let alone being found within minutes.

The other question is, how does she kill this thing? Cleary, she had never seen a creature like this. Is it human? She pretty much knows the answer to that is no. But what is it, then? Even though her mind tried to rationalize away the several bullets that the creature had taken; she knows, deep down, that something is different about him. At first, she wrote off his creepy, grotesque looks and deformities to years of isolation and depravity. But as time went on, and with more interactions; it was becoming more evident that things just weren't adding up to the creature being human. But still, she believed she could kill the beast. Certainly, a head shot would do it! What other options did she have? Cognitive dissonance was the only thing that was keeping her going.

The Power's Within

She ran as fast as she could back to the cabin. All of the night's events raced through her head, even faster than she was running. She passed Fisher Ave, and was soon back at the cabin. She remembered that Harry had put the full bullet clip in his back, left pocket. The thought of seeing Harry dead and up close made her dizzy. But she had to keep moving forward. And she had to get that clip.

She approaches Harry's body apprehensively. Tears immediately flood her eyes when she gets a look at his mangled body. Like the others, Harry's guts had been ripped out and a bone was missing from his leg. She also sees the creature's dirty, bloody bag of bones not far from Harry's body. She anxiously reaches into his pocket. She grabs hold of the clip and loads the weapon. The moment the clip snaps in place, she hears fast-approaching footsteps. It's the creature sprinting in her direction.

He was approximately 40-yards away,

and coming from the direction of Fisher Ave. Instead of lining up a shot, Laurie decides it would be best to get him in close quarters for the sake of accuracy. 'Her only hope,' she thinks, 'is a direct headshot.' After all, she has always been a fan of those zombie movies.

Laurie sprints for the front door of the cabin. She pushes the door in and closes it behind her. She slides the couch in front of the door to block entry. She lights two candles and sits in the corner of the living room. She slows her breathing and focuses on her hearing. Her eyes are wide open. She is barely blinking. She tries to calm herself and stop herself from shaking. A steady trigger hand will be essential to her survival. That's when she hears a loud *THUD* coming from the family room. Then, complete silence again.

She waits with bated breath for the creature to show himself. She looks closely in the direction of the hallway, but she doesn't see or hear anything. She slowly rises to her feet. She can no longer sit and wait. It was time to face her fears. Laurie walks gingerly toward the hallway.

However, as she does so, the creature silently climbs down from the ceiling above her head. Laurie has no idea that the creature had entered through the secret entrance on the second-floor and scaled the ceiling to get to her. He was above her waiting to strike just before she stood to her feet.

He walks silently behind her waiting for the right moment. It is as though he wants to savor this kill. Afterall, this is his last victim. Before these kills, the creature hadn't killed in a year. Not because he didn't want to, but because he didn't have the right opportunity. Laurie continues forward, still not aware she is the one being hunted.

Suddenly, Laurie hears the floor creak behind her. She spins around quickly, pointing the gun in the ready position. But nothing is there. The creature is out of sight, again. She turns back and continues forward. She approaches the foyer. She takes a breath before entering the dining room. She holds her arms out stiffly as she makes the sharp turn. She holds the gun with both hands and sways it side to side with the movement of her eyes.

Again, Laurie hears a loud *thud* from behind. It appears someone was running up the stairs. She froze and listened. The footsteps went from the stairs to the ceiling above. Laurie looks up and squints her eyes. Someone is walking around the creaky floor above. Laurie reroutes her course and heads to the stairs.

Before taking a step, Laurie looks up the stairs. She sees nothing. She slowly creeps up, expecting an ambush at any moment. Every step is agonizing. She replays every scenario in her head. Some of those do not turn out so well. She tries to remain positive. She quickly scratches any of the negative attack scenarios and focuses on the positive ones. She begins to reinforce the dominance in her mind. This helps her gain confidence.

Laurie enters the hallway. She is moving slower now. She has become the hunter. In her mind, she is sure she will win this battle. Fear left her. She is hungry for revenge. She is eager to end this for good! She enters the second-bedroom. She searches cautiously, but nothing is there.

She proceeds to the master bedroom. A bit of fear creeps in all of a sudden. 'He has to be here,' she thinks. The inexorable moment of truth and confrontation is only seconds away. But still she holds steadfast to her position.

She slowly opens the door to the master bedroom. She opens it halfway and scans the room with her pistol. She walks in a few steps and realizes that there is no one there. 'Where did he go?' she thought. The door closes abruptly. Hiding behind the door is the creature.

He attacks before she can process the situation. She raises the gun halfway, but the creature is on her before she can take aim.

Smack!

He knocks the gun away from her and backhands her across the left side of her face. The gun flies under the bed. Laurie flew into the closet door. She drops to the ground. She loses consciousness momentarily. She regains her senses just in time to see the monster grab her by the hair with his left hand and raise her forcefully to a standing position. Laurie is helpless. She is now at the mercy of the beast. He revels in her fear and her vulnerability. His hot, rotting breath overwhelms her senses. She can only breath it in and hope that she can be desensitized, at best, to the rancid smell. The beast sticks the claw from his right-index finger into her stomach. Laurie gasps and groans.

He looks at her as a primitive being. She is prey. He has no fear that she can harm him in any way. If he thought she could, she would have been dead a long time ago. He lets go of her hair. Her feet finally touch the ground again. He backs up a bit. She slumps over in pain. He wants a challenge. Laurie grabs a porcelain statue off the night stand and attempts to swing it at him. It was a slow, weak attempt. The creature slaps it out of her hand before she can even get it above her waste. He is toying with her. Taunting her.

Laurie screams in frustration: Her voice suddenly changes. In the *Nahuatl* tongue she screams, *"Tlanhuizxixinia!"* *("I disarm you!").*

The beast suddenly seemed

confused. He backs up a bit and lets out a distressful, screeching sound. It is as if he has lost control of his bodily functions. Laurie uses the opportunity to make a strategic move. She bends down and dives under the bed. She grabs the gun. She emerges from underneath the bed. The monster is still in an almost frozen state. He looks confused, but also very angry and desperate. She aims the gun at his head.

BANG!

One shot to the forehead drops him, cold. Laurie pauses. She is in shock. The creature is down and not moving. She had done it! She releases the gun from her hand. She drops it in dramatic fashion. She is exhausted. She walks around the bed, almost in a daze. She now feels the pain in her stomach. She sits on the right edge of the bed, facing the door. The creature is lying motionless behind her, on the floor, by the left side of the bed.

Laurie tries to gather herself. She begins assessing the damage to her stomach. She puts her hand on her stomach and raises it. Her hand is full of blood. She has nothing left. She almost thought of leaning backwards and just falling asleep right there. But her mouth is dry. She needs water. She rises from the bed, slowly. As she takes a step toward the door, the monster somehow rises again to a standing position.

Laurie turns, inadvertently, to see the creature rising. Not only is he still alive, he looks refreshed. He stuck out his chest. His eyes, piercing. It was as if he had taken that fall only to demoralize his victim with his rise. Laurie's body went from near shut down back to survival mode. Her heartbeat shot up, instantly. She ran for her life. Down the stairs and out of the house. The creature gave chase. He remained very close behind.

This time, Laurie makes a left after exiting the cabin. She runs along the fence of the farm land, toward the helipad. She is now crying profusely and out of answers. She is hopeless. As she passes the church, she realizes there is nowhere left to run. She turns and just stands there. Something inside of her seems to snap. The creature is soon in her site. He slows his run to a walk once her sees her immobilized.

The creature pauses and gawks at her for a moment. This is it. The creature had, had enough of the games. It was time for him to end this; to go in for the kill.

The monster's knees bend slightly. He springs forward and aggressively charges. Laurie scowls. She stands her ground. She swings both elbows back, fixing both hands into a claw-like shape. With the monster quickly approaching, she forcefully thrusts both her hands forward and shouts [again in the mysterious Nahuatl tongue],

"*Aamaque. Notzonquiscatlanahuatil!*" ("*Go Away. I command you!*").

At that moment, a large, round, transparent light emanates from each of her hands. The lights shoot forward quickly toward the creature. As it makes impact, it also appears to trigger a sonic *BOOM*, that levels the surrounding area. Nothing within a twenty-yard radius is sparred. As trees buckle, so too do Laurie and the monster.

Both are sent flying backwards—both of their feet swinging forward ninety-degrees— from the impact of the blast. And then, complete darkness.

A Familiar Voice

A glimmer of light can be seen, even though very blurry. Laurie's eyes struggle to open. Clear sounds are replaced by only muffled, distorted audio. The sky is filled with light. She is groggy. She has no idea where she is or what has happened. A vision of the monster charging her is all she can remember. As her eyes open wider, they meet the blinding sun. Laurie covers her eyes with her right hand to block it out.

"H-H-H," a voice screams in the distance. Laurie is too groggy to make out the words. She's not even sure the voice is real. Or what is real, for that matter.

"H-E-Y," the voice screams again, as it gets closer. This time she is able to understand. Still, she lay motionless on her back.

"Hey, little lady." It's Dizzy! He stands over her, and then kneels beside her.

"Are you okay? What are you doing down there?"

Laurie has so many thoughts. But the words escape before they can enter her mouth. Dizzy grabs her arm and Laurie uses his grip to boost herself up. The first thing she does is look around for the monster.

He's gone!

Was it all just a dream?

"Where are the others?" asks Dizzy. Laurie shakes her head side to side, slowly. A glaze still covering her bleary eyes.

****

Laurie suddenly awakens! She abruptly and anxiously sits up. She is on a gurney. Through the window she can see Dizzy talking to a military officer and a man in a long white hospital coat right outside her room. Dizzy looks in and gives a faint smile and a half-hearted wave. Dizzy shakes hands with the military officer and is soon out of sight. The man in the white coat enters the room. She looks at his name-tag, which reads: *Dr. Hernandez.*

"Where am I?" Laurie asks anxiously.

"You are safe now," he says. "You've been through quite the ordeal; I've been told by your friend. You should rest."

"I need to make a phone call, I need

to notify my family," Laurie says. She stands up. Two orderlies walk in the room.

"Now, now," the doctor says, "you need to rest now."

One orderly grabs her left arm. The other grabs her right.

"Wait a minute!" she shouts. "Let go of me!" She is confused as to why she is being treated this way. As they hold her firmly, the doctor pops the cap off of the needle with his mouth and sticks a needle into her arm. Within seconds, Laurie is asleep. The doctor leaves the room and reconvenes with the military officer.

"She is asleep for now," the doctor says. "We will keep her here for evaluation as long as necessary."

"Good," says the military officer. "We cannot have any of this get out or go public."

****

Back in Pavoso, an owl soars through the air. Flying over the woods, he is headed directly for the mine. The owl swoops down toward the ground. And just before he

lands, he physically transforms into-
-*THE MONSTER!*

A flawless transition, as his feet touch down and he begins walking. A menacing scowl is all he wears, as no doubt, he is angrier than ever that for the first time someone has survived his onslaught!

THE END

To be continued...

"The Whistling Man II" will be available some time in 2021.

For all things "Whistling Man," or to get exclusive deals and Whistling Man 2 release dates and content, please visit:

https://thewhistlingman-savive.com/